forbidden Soldier

N ENGLISH CIVIL WAR LOVE STORY

ALISON PRINCE

SCHOLASTIC

While the events described and some of the characters in this book may be based on actual historical events and real people, this story is a work of fiction.

Scholastic Children's Books
Euston House, 24 Eversholt Street,
London, NW1 1DB, UK

A division of Scholastic Ltd
London ~ New York ~ Toronto ~ Sydney ~ Auckland
Mexico City ~ New Delhi ~ Hong Kong

Published in the UK by Scholastic Ltd, 2014

Text copyright © Alison Prince, 2014
Cover photography copyright © Jeff Cottenden, 2014

ISBN 978 1407 13888 6

The right of Alison Prince and Jeff Cottenden to be identified as the author and cover photographer of this work has been asserted by them in accordance with the Copyright, Designs and Patents Act, 1988.

CHRISTMAS BANNED

We have just finished morning prayers. I am going with the others to breakfast in the kitchen, but my father stops me. "Just a minute, Hannah."

When Mama and my brothers and sisters have left, he goes on, "There is something I need to say to you. You are not a child. You are fourteen years old. Many girls are married at such an age. Some have children of their own."

Does he mean I *should* be married? I have never thought of it. The idea shocks me a little.

Papa says, "Don't look so alarmed. I have no desire to see you leave the house – your mother values your help. But I would like to see you behaving more responsibly. When you were getting the little ones dressed this morning, I heard you prattling to them about the coming Christmas as though looking forward to a mere – *revel.*" He speaks the word with distaste. "The birth of Jesus, may I remind you, is no excuse for greed and self-indulgence."

I'd never thought it was, but it is better not to say anything. I stare down at my linked hands, tightly gripped in front of my white apron.

"Do you understand what I am saying?" Papa demands. "Look at me!"

I meet his fierce eyes under the bushy eyebrows and stammer, "I am sorry, Papa. I just thought – Christmas is Christ's birthday. To be celebrated."

He snorts with disapproval.

"That is the Catholic excuse. But their worship of the Virgin Mary and the birth in the stable is mistaken. You must remember, Hannah, Mary was merely a woman. A good woman, undoubtedly, meek and pure – but not holy in her own right. She was fortunate in being chosen by Almighty God to bear His son."

I whisper, "Yes, Papa."

His words give me a terrible sense of loss. Mary has always seemed so gentle and kind, sitting there among the donkeys and oxen with the Christ child in her arms. She seems – or used to seem – easier to understand than God Himself, who is so vast and remote.

Papa has more to say.

"This is 1647, Hannah. We are modern men and women. As Puritans, we understand the truth. Pure obedience to the will of God needs no paintings or statues, no bells or tinsel or ribbons, no feasting and singing of noisy songs. God does not need to be depicted or explained. He needs no sweetening. The Scottish Presbyterian Church has banned all revels at Christmas, and our English Parliament is now doing likewise."

He frowns as another thought strikes him.

"The Scots are reputed to celebrate the New Year in a regrettably Pagan way, with excesses of whisky and profane music, but that is probably only in the wilder parts. Some of their tribes are still very uncivilized."

I don't see why he is talking about Scotland. We live in Canterbury, in the county of Kent. It's as far from Scotland as anyone can get. Mama says France is closer, though we can't see it, just across the sea from Dover. Her brother is a fisherman, so he has seen it sometimes. France is a Catholic country. Our King Charles married the French king's daughter.

Papa is irked by my silence.

"Have you been listening to what I am saying?"

"Yes, Papa. I was just thinking about France being closer than Scotland. And Queen Henrietta Maria being French."

"Were you, indeed?" He looks at me with curiosity. "Then you might like to know that King Charles refuses to recognize the legal Parliament of England. He says he has absolute power to rule. He can do no wrong."

"But all of us can do wrong."

Papa gives me an approving smile. "Exactly," he says. "Now go along and get your breakfast, Hannah. But remember – I will hear no more of this silly chatter to your brothers about Christmas."

"No, Papa. I am sorry."

I drop him a curtsey and stand back to let him go out before me.

Being the eldest girl of seven children keeps me busy, especially now that Mama is pregnant again. She often stands with her hands pressed to her back as though it is aching, and I worry about her and help as much as I can. Little Leah is not a year old yet and still suckling, and Jeffrey at almost three is one of those active children who needs a lot of attention. He learned to walk early, and then to run and to climb, and James calls him "a right little monkey". James, the eldest of us, is seventeen. He helps my father in his saddlery business, cutting and stitching leather and forging iron for stirrups and harness buckles.

I should have had an elder sister, but she died of a fever when she was only a few months old. Mama said she was called Margaret. So there is a three-year gap between James and me. Elizabeth was born just a year later, then my two younger brothers, Will and Michael. They go to school, as James did, but Elizabeth and I do not. Mama never learned to read, but it does not bother her – she says she has enough to do without books as well. But I always wanted to know what the letters meant, so I began to puzzle them out, and Papa seemed surprised and quite pleased, so he helped me.

I taught Elizabeth to read while we were both still quite small. It is a joy to her, for she was born with a twisted foot and cannot get out and about as the rest of us do. She is good at needlework and mending and helps Mama with the cooking, but she can only move slowly, leaning on a crutch. She cannot fetch water or peg clothes on the line, let alone roam through the woods and fields as I do. Going into Canterbury is a rare treat for her, and only happens when Papa has a horse harnessed to the trap and is not too busy to take her with him. But she reads everything she can lay her hands on.

Will and Michael are home from school now because Christmas is coming. Mama gives them jobs to do around the house, but they are bored, of course.

This morning, Michael wants to go to the market.

"Yes, let's!" says Will. "Can we, Hannah? Please!"

Jeffrey is jumping up and down and shouting some kind of song. Mama is chopping leeks and potatoes to make soup for our dinner. She rests her knife on the table in one hand, the other pressed to her back.

"Do take them out, Hannah," she says. "Give me a little peace."

Elizabeth says, "I'll finish these vegetables, Mama. Why don't you sit down for a while?"

My mother doesn't answer, just goes on chopping. She is like the house martins that nest under our eaves and fly

5

all day to catch the dancing gnats. They never stop flying except to roost, because if they do, they will drop out of the sky.

Mama leaves the knife on the table and fetches her purse from the dresser drawer. "Get me some raisins from the grocer's shop," she says. "And some sugar. Oh, and take the little pan with you – the one that lost its handle last week. If the tinsmith is in the market, ask him if he can mend it."

Elizabeth has finished chopping the onion Mama left on the board. She reaches for another one.

I set out with Will and Michael. Jeffrey is running ahead of us. White frost lies in the narrow alleys between the houses that the winter sun has not yet touched. Their leaning upper storeys are close enough for people to talk or argue across the gap between their facing windows. There is no sky to be seen except a narrow strip of it between the roofs. It's useful on rainy days, because you can walk almost everywhere in the shelter of the buildings and not get wet, but this morning I'm impatient to get out into the winter sun.

Jeffrey is pretending to be a young horse, galloping and whinnying. I will not scold him, though Papa would disapprove of such behaviour. Mama says boys too young to work need to use their energy or it turns to mischief, and she is right, as she is about so many things.

The spires of the Cathedral rise above the house roofs, so tall that they can be seen everywhere. Those of us who know the town never have to think about getting lost in the narrow streets, but strangers often do, so they find the spires useful. Quite a lot of strangers come to Canterbury, for the Cathedral is the shrine of St Thomas à Becket, who was killed there by the soldiers of Henry the Second, many years ago. Papa said Becket sought his own martyrdom and does not merit such worship. There is so much that I don't understand.

The market place is crowded, of course. Housewives are laying in food for Christmas, which is only three days away. There is little left in the gardens now except root crops and winter cabbage or kale, so people are jostling round the stalls.

"Look!" says Michael. "There's the town crier."

The big man in his red coat and cocked hat climbs the two steps to the stone mounting block outside the inn so everyone can see him. He rings his bell for attention and shouts, "Oyez! Oyez!" A crowd is gathering, waiting to hear what news he has. He unrolls his official parchment.

"Oyez!" he bellows again. "Hear ye! A proclamation from the Master Mayor!"

Every head turns to look, like trout facing upstream. The crier holds up his parchment and gives it an important flourish, then starts reading from it in his loud voice.

"Christmas is forbidden! By order of Parliament, Christmas is to be done away with!"

Shouts of protest drown his voice as he goes on reading.

Will and Michael have wriggled their way to the front of the crowd and Jeffrey is trying to join them. I hold his hand tightly as we edge between people. We must keep together if there is going to be trouble – and to judge from the shouts and grumbles, there well may be.

The crier's face is as red as his coat as he bawls the rest of his message, speaking the official words slowly.

"It has been declared that Christmas Day and all other superstitious festivals are to be put down. Shops and businesses will not close on Saturday 25th December. A market will be held as usual."

There is a fresh roar of anger, though a few dark-clad Puritans in the crowd nod in approval, as my father would.

The crier rolls his parchment up and steps down from the mounting block, moving on to deliver his message to the next place on his list, ringing his bell and calling, "Oyez, oyez!"

"What does 'Oyez' mean?" Will asks.

Papa told me, so I know.

"It's from a French word that means 'Hear'. So it really does mean, 'Hear ye', like he said."

All round us people are complaining furiously.

8

A woman asks of nobody in particular, "Where is it all going to end?"

"Bad enough when they closed the theatres," her friend agrees. "Shocking, that. Actors getting whipped if they were caught performing, and everyone in the audience fined five shillings. Five *shillings!* Where would we get that kind of money?"

A man has climbed up on the mounting block where the crier stood.

"This Parliament has gone too far," he shouts. "We'd be better off with the King."

His friends roar agreement. Fists are shaken. A rhythmic chant starts to build up.

"Bring back the King!"

"Bring back the King!"

A man in a plain black coat shouts in reply, "Charles is useless. He could not run a market stall!"

His supporters cheer him, but others boo and shout. A man pushes him hard and he staggers and almost falls. One of his friends turns on the pushing man, who has long, curly hair, and smacks him in the face, then gets hit by someone else. All round us a fight is breaking out. Sticks are flailing as well as fists. Women are screaming. There is blood pouring from the curly-haired man's nose.

I must get the boys out of here. I tighten my grip on Jeffrey's hand and shout to Will and Michael, "Keep close!"

We start to work our way out of the crowd, but a tangle of battling men almost runs us down. We duck away as best we can.

Shepherding the boys out of the market, I think of what Papa would say – that the objectors are a rabble of Royalists who are disobeying a law passed by the Parliament. And he would be right. But, as the woman asked, where is it all going to end?

At last we are out of the square. I can't go back to find the tinsmith, but the grocer's shop is open, so I can get the sugar and raisins.

Papa is reading his Bible. Elizabeth is sitting near him to share the light of his candle, as she is sewing a button on a shirt. Mama went to bed after our evening meal, saying she was very tired. She took baby Leah with her. She has stopped feeding her now the next baby is coming, but Leah has not taken easily to milk from a cup, and is fretful. Will and Michael have been in their bed since about six, and James is dozing in a chair by the fire, tired after a day of helping in the workshop.

My mind is full of questions about what happened in the market.

"Papa," I venture, "forgive me for disturbing you, but can I ask you something?"

He puts his finger on the page to mark his place and looks up.

"Yes, Hannah. What is it?"

"There was a fight in the market today, because Christmas has been forbidden. People were shouting that they want the King back in power. Do you think that will happen?"

His mouth tightens. "It must not happen. England has a legal Parliament. It can pass laws and govern the country. We have no need for a stupid and arrogant king."

"But – what if the King will not go?"

Papa gives up trying to keep his place in the Bible and closes it.

"He will *have* to go. He has caused one war already, and we fear there will be another."

"How did he cause a war?"

Papa sighs, but remains patient.

"He and Archbishop Laud tried to make the Scots use a new English prayer book. They took it to Edinburgh and told the Dean of the Cathedral it must be used throughout his country. But the Scots would not have it. The new book is very close to the old Catholic liturgy, and they objected. When the Dean began to read from it, he was shouted down."

"*Shouted* – in the *Cathedral?*"

I am amazed. Our Cathedral is hushed and quiet – not that I've been in there often, as we have our own Puritan church, small and plain.

James has woken up and he laughs.

"They did more than shout," he says. "They threw chairs

and overturned the communion table – started a riot. All over Scotland, it was the same. A bishop tried to read from the new book with a pair of loaded pistols by the lectern, but the congregation rioted all the same."

"Is it still going on?"

"Yes, indeed," Papa says. "They have drawn up a National Covenant." He holds up a hand to forestall my next question. "The Covenant is a promise never to accept the English Prayer Book. Thousands of Presbyterian Scots have signed it."

"King Charles got it so wrong," James says. "He thought he could bring the Scots in on his side, but caused a war instead – and lost it. The Covenanting army beat him in every battle. He blamed Archbishop Laud, of course. Had him executed. After all those years of being his right-hand man."

"Ugh, horrible. Are we still at war with the Scots?"

"Not at the moment," Papa says. "After the final battle, Charles surrendered to the Presbyterian army. They took him to Hampton Court. He promised he would stay there, but he broke his word. Just a month ago, he escaped in the middle of the night."

"Where did he go?"

"To the Isle of Wight. He thought the governor of the island would protect him."

James is laughing again. "And what a mistake that was!" he says. "The governor locked him up in Carisbrooke Castle."

"Is he still there?"

"Oh, yes," says James. Nobody gets out of that place. And if they did, it's on an island, so they wouldn't get far."

"Despite that," Papa says, "Charles still plans to return to power."

Which brings me back to my first question.

"But *can* he?"

Papa sighs.

"The danger is, Hannah, that he may make a deal with the Scots. If they will attack England and reclaim the throne for him, he might promise that Scottish Presbyterianism would be the official religion of England."

I'm confused all over again. Presbyterians are Protestants. Puritans are Protestants, too.

"Wouldn't that be good?"

"Definitely not," Papa says. "Charles would immediately abolish the English Parliament. He would be the absolute ruler again."

"And we'd all use the new prayer book?"

James snorts in derision.

"We could use whatever we liked, as long as he is king. We could worship a donkey for all he'd care."

Papa says, "This is no laughing matter, James. England will have no peace until the King is brought to see sense."

That is what I am trying to find out.

"What if he does not see sense?"

My father's lips tighten. "Then," he says, "Parliament may

have to condemn him to death. But I hope it will not come to that."

He opens his Bible again, finds his place and goes on reading.

HOLLY AND MUSKETS

It is Christmas morning, but we have been careful to show no excitement. We gathered in the front room for prayers then had breakfast, and Papa has gone across the yard to his workshop as usual.

A little furtively, we have given each other small gifts. Elizabeth and I did lots of secret sewing, and so did Mama, so there were new shirts for the boys and fresh white caps to exchange between ourselves. I knitted warm mittens for Mama, and she loves them. James carved a boat for Jeffrey, even though he thinks Papa is right, and Mama made him a puppet out of some grey cloth left from a dress. It has furry paws at the end of its arms and a rabbit's head that Michael carved from pale wood. Its loose fabric body fits over Jeffrey's small hand, and he loves it. He waves its little arms with his thumb and forefinger and says it is called Ned.

Papa was adamant that he wanted no presents, but I wanted to give him something, if I could find a gift that would not annoy him. I took a scrap of leather from the waste bin in his workshop and shaped it into a narrow bookmark, then stitched a plain cross on it in black thread.

I have not given it to him yet. I'm standing at the door of his workshop, which is open because he is firing up the forge, but I can't find the courage to go in. What if he thinks the bookmark is sinful?

He has seen me.

"Yes, Hannah, what is it?"

I give him the bookmark and say, "It is not a celebration, Papa. It's just to keep your place in the Bible."

He considers it carefully, then nods.

"Thank you, Hannah. Yes. It is a useful thing."

He puts the bookmark carefully behind a pair of heavy cutters.

"Now go back to the others," he says. "You will get your dress dirty in here."

Mama knows from my smile that the gift has been accepted, and she kisses me.

She says to all of us, "You must remember that your father loves you. He may seem stern sometimes, but it is only because he wants you to grow up as people who will work hard and be respected."

We know her words are true. But we also know we have to be careful.

After dinner Will and Michael go out into the lane to bowl the iron hoops that James made for them. They take Jeffrey and his puppet with them. Mama is sitting by the fire, and for once, she has slipped into a doze. Elizabeth is busy with her embroidery. James is in the workshop with Papa.

I'm prickling with curiosity about what will have happened in Canterbury on this forbidden Christmas Day. Will people have obeyed the instruction to hold a market as usual, and kept their shops open? After all the protests, it seems impossible – but I so much want to know. Since the boys are happy and occupied, I could slip away and have a quick look. I'd be back in half an hour, and nobody would miss me. Very quietly, I take my shawl and bonnet from the peg.

Elizabeth is watching. I put a finger to my lips, and she nods.

I go out, closing the door silently behind me. I can hear the rattle of the boys' hoops over the cobbles from an alleyway behind the houses, and their shouts and laughter. I set out along the path that goes the other way, towards the town.

It seems odd to carry no shopping basket and have no coins in my pocket. I am here alone for the first time, for no reason but sheer curiosity. Papa would forbid it if he knew, for it is sinful self-indulgence. Although – or because – I am empty-handed, I feel burdened with guilt. But I keep walking.

The market traders have ignored the Mayor's order to turn up as usual. The square is empty but for an old woman standing beside a bag of muddy carrots, holding up two live, skinny chickens with their legs tied together. But in the main street, several of the shops are open. And there is a rumpus going on.

A crowd of men has stormed into the grocer's shop. They are shouting at its owner that Christmas is a holy day and he must put up his shutters.

"I have no choice," he protests. "I will be fined unless I open my shop."

"You *do* have a choice," the leader of the men shouts at him. "You can choose to obey the Parliament or not, and you have chosen wrong. You should obey the law of God, not some jumped-up human authority. I tell you now – close this shop and go home to your family to celebrate the birth of Christ. Close it right now, or we will close it for you."

The men are of course Royalists. Their collars are lace-edged, and their uncut hair is shoulder-long. James says they took this style because when the King was imprisoned, he would not let anyone near him with scissors or a razor. One can hardly blame him – the head and the throat are very close, and he did not know who could be trusted. So his supporters, "Cavaliers" as they are called, wear their hair long, too, and look very different from the close-cropped, plainly dressed Puritans.

The grocer is wringing his hands in anguish.

"But it is the law of England," he says, "I must do as the Parliament has ordered."

"You should be ashamed, peddling goods and making money on Christ's birthday!" one of the Royalists yells – to cheers from the others.

"It is not my fault, I cannot—"

The Cavalier leader loses patience. He slaps the man across the face with his gloved hand and shouts at him, "You are wrong. You must obey the law of God, not of the Parliament."

"I am afraid of what they will do," the grocer whimpers, and there is a shout of derisive laughter.

"You should be more afraid of us," the leader says. He swings round and adds, "Right, boys. Teach this man a lesson."

They are like dogs let off the lead.

One of them grabs a ham that lies on a slab and hurls it into the street, where the crowd that has gathered starts to fight over it. Another kicks over a barrel of pickled herrings that spill across the floor. A third jumps across the counter and tips up the big block of butter standing on its marble shelf, hurling it to the floor.

The grocer's wife screams. Her husband tries to push an attacker away, but a punch in the face sends him staggering back, and he trips over a barrel and lands with his feet in the air. The attackers are slashing sacks open with their swords. Flour and oatmeal pour out. They kick a barrel of apples into the street, where children rush to grab them then run away, shrieking with fear and excitement. A side of bacon is hauled from its hook and thrown onto the cobbles. Knives are out – people are hacking pieces off it as fast as they can.

Some bystanders try to help the grocer and his wife but

far more people are looting from the ransacked shop. They squabble and fight among themselves over the spilled goods even as the destruction goes on. I've backed away across the street, but keep watching in a terrible kind of fascination. Owners of the other shops that had opened are quickly barring their doors and putting up their shutters, but a couple of Royalists holding flaming brands above their heads are running from one shop to the next, thrusting the flares in wherever they can. A woman shrieks as they charge into her drapery shop where lengths of cloth hang on display at the door. They burst into flames at once.

A basket of eggs crashes onto the cobbles in front of me, splashing my skirt, and I suddenly realize that I am in danger. I turn and run, holding my shawl across my face against the spark-laden smoke billowing across the square. But I've left it too late. A squad of armed, mounted men is clattering over the cobbles towards me, the Mayor himself at its head. William Bridge. I know his name but I have never seen him. I cram myself into a doorway in the narrow street to let them pass.

The Mayor yells at the battling crowd, "Stop this disorder at once! Go back to your homes!"

Few people hear him, and those who do take no notice. Mr Bridge dismounts and strides forward, swinging a heavy cudgel. He strikes a man across the head, felling him to his knees, and shouts at the rampaging people again, still expecting to be obeyed – but the mob overwhelms him like a tide of floodwater and he goes down, lost to view. His men, at a barked order from their sergeant, level their muskets and fire. The noise is deafening – I clap my hands over my ears. People have fallen, but in the drifting, acrid musket smoke I am half blinded and can't see much. *This is God's punishment*, my mind tells me. *You should not be here.*

I must get home. I'm running down the alleyway that leads to Burgate, but there's another mob blocking the end, and more soldiers. I duck down a different alley and keep going, turning whichever way is open. I come out near Wingate – but people are barricading it. They've got an overturned cart and an iron bedstead, and are hauling anything they can find into place – tree branches, a table, logs, buckets, planks. If the soldiers are coming up behind me I'll be trapped in a fight. I could die here. I will never see Mama and Elizabeth again. I am weeping with terror.

A woman sees me and says, "You want to get out, dear?"

"Yes!"

She yells at the men, "Let this girl through!"

They make a small gap and beckon.

"Over here – be quick!"

I squeeze between them then pick up my skirts and run. I go on running until I am nearly to the top of the long hill and gasping for breath, then pause and look back, panting hard. Smoke is rising from the town in a wavering column, and I can still hear the rattle of guns and a tumult of voices, thin and clear in the distance, like the chattering of starlings. I rub my hot face on my sleeve. My clothes smell of musket smoke. I go on, more slowly. Ahead of me, the afternoon sun hangs low behind the bare trees. I have been out much longer than I meant, and because I came out of the wrong gate, I am on the far side of the woods.

It is quiet among the trees. A small stream runs by the path. I pull a handful of grass and dip it in the water, then wipe the spatter of egg from my skirt. The wet cloth will have dried by the time I get home. Some kind of calm starts to return. These woods are familiar – we come here to gather firewood. I start picking up useful-sized twigs as I go along, but am guilty about that, too, because it is an excuse. I can hear the conversation already.

"What have you been doing, Hannah?"

"Gathering firewood, Papa."

I have never in my life needed any excuse. I have always been free to come and go, but on this Christmas Day I sneaked out to do something that would not have been approved. And now I am gathering branches because I dare not tell my father the truth.

I am a coward. And because I am a coward, I am going to be a wordless liar.

Doing a wrong thing tangles you like burdock, clinging to everything it touches. The unwieldy bundle of sticks gets heavier as I walk and I need both arms to steady it on my shoulder. My back aches, but I am glad of this small punishment.

The wood gives way to the meadow that slopes down to our house. It was fenced last year so I have a stile to climb over. Even from this distance, I can hear the ring of Papa's hammer strokes, as clear in the cold air as the sound of a high, small bell striking regular time. I feel a rush of love for him. He is so steady. So obedient to the service of God through the use of his hands and mind. A good man.

Stars are appearing in the darkening sky. Because it is Christmas I think of that star over the stable where Christ was born – but Mary was just a woman, Papa says. We must not love the scent of green boughs in the house and the taste of apples stored since the autumn for this special day. I love and respect my father, but it grieves me to lose that thrilling sense of wonder, and I cannot silence a small voice of doubt. Christmas has always seemed innocent and good, as I, on this Christmas Day, am not.

Is this thought a sin?

I do not know.

The ring of hammer on anvil gets louder as I near the house. The news of what has happened in Canterbury will be louder than this by tomorrow morning.

I put my bundle of firewood in the barn as quietly as I can, but Papa knows I am here. He comes across from his workshop and frowns.

"I see you have been working at a useful task, Hannah," he says. "But you should not be out on your own with darkness coming. It is not seemly for a young woman. I would prefer that you take one of your brothers with you."

"Yes, Papa. I am sorry."

Far more sorry than he knows. I have a desperate moment of wishing I could tell him where I have been and what I have seen, but my courage fails. I follow him into the house and say nothing.

SPILT MILK

This morning, everything seems normal. Mama is making bread, and Elizabeth is cutting up onions and potatoes for soup. Nobody has come to the house yet, so yesterday's riot in the town remains my secret.

Jeffrey is running about with his puppet, picking things up with its paws and shouting in a squeaky rabbit voice, "Want grass! Want grass!"

He needs exercise. It is a perfect excuse for another journey into the town, this time on a legitimate errand. When I come back, I can report what has happened and say what I have seen today. Yesterday's evasion will not matter any more, and can be forgotten.

"Shall I take him out?" I suggest in disgraceful innocence. "We need some milk."

Mama is grateful. "Yes, do that," she says. "I scalded the churn, so it's ready."

We had a cow when we shared the common land for grazing, but the meadows all belong to one big farmer now, and we have to buy milk.

Jeffrey and I set out. He rabbit-hops happily along,

25

making Ned the puppet nip at the ivy leaves growing along the wall.

Hannah, you are not a child, Papa said. An argument starts in my mind.

I am old enough to be a man's wife. Jeffrey could almost be my son, not my brother.

If I have reached such maturity, am I not old enough to make up my own mind where I go, and when and why?

Yes, perhaps. And yet – there are things about being grown-up that I don't want to face. I was with Mama in those long hours when Leah was being born, and though she never cried out, she writhed and gasped, and I could see the pain was terrible. When I went out to wet a cloth to wipe her face, the midwife came to join me at the well. She said, "The child is very big, Hannah. This will not be easy for your mother." I knew it was a warning that Mama might die. Yet when she cradled her new baby, all the pain and struggle seemed forgotten. She looked blissful, but I don't know if I could find it blissful.

Jeffrey stops suddenly. "Soldiers!" he says.

Ahead of us, men armed with halberds and muskets are guarding the gate. They are Protestant troops, wearing breastplates and the plain, round helmets that make people call them Roundheads. Jeffrey is thrilled. He starts to run towards them, but I grab his hand and pull him back. Guilt strikes all over again. I should not have brought him. I've made him part of my excuse, God forgive me. The guards are stopping everyone and asking their business. The Mayor and Alderman are watching, looking very official and severe.

"I don't know if we can get milk today," I tell Jeffrey. "We may not be able to go in. Mind – there's a cab coming."

We step aside and stand on the grass verge as a horse pulling a hackney cab trots up. The captain of the guard steps forward to halt it.

"Name?" he barks at the driver, who sits with a rug over his knees against the cold. He has brown hair that curls over the collar of his thick coat.

"Joyce," he answers.

The Roundhead captain sneers. "Joyce? What kind of a name is that?"

The cabman's mouth tightens, and his chin goes up.

"A decent name," he says, then adds with deliberation, "Good enough for a filthy Roundhead."

The captain does not reply, but snatches his musket to his shoulder and fires. The driver slumps sideways. People scream and yell protest. The cabman's young horse is trembling between the shafts, tossing its head. Its eyes are rolling, showing white rims. It doesn't know what to do. The reins are slack in the driver's dangling hand, so it has no guidance. It makes small, uneasy, dancing steps and its ears have flattened. At any minute, it may bolt. I try to move back out of the way with Jeffrey, but the crowd has surged in behind us, blocking the way to retreat. People are shaking their fists and yelling abuse at the army captain, even though there is a risk that he may shoot again.

"Murderer!" a woman screams at him. "You've killed an innocent man!"

Blood is soaking through the sleeve of the driver's coat, but he is not dead. With one hand he is tugging feebly at the reins, trying to turn the horse, but the crowd is too angry to notice. They have surrounded the Mayor and Alderman, raining blows on them. People are grabbing stones from the road's edge and hurling them at the soldiers. One of them strikes the cabman's horse hard on the rump and it flings up its head and turns fast. It is coming straight for us.

"Jeffrey, *mind*—!"

My head hurts.

"She's coming to," someone says.

"Jeffrey, mind – Jeffrey, *mind*!"

It's my voice. Strange.

I can't seem to move.

There is a hand under my shoulder. Someone is helping me to sit up.

"Your little boy is all right," a man's voice says, close to me. "He's here, look."

Jeffrey is being fussed over by the people standing round

us. He is crying. He must be hurt. I'm struggling to get up but my limbs feel as weak as water and it is strangely difficult.

"Don't worry," the man beside me says. "He isn't hurt. He's just cross."

Jeffrey is pushing his rabbit puppet into my face, weeping with fury.

"Horse trod on Ned! *Bad* horse!"

The puppet's head has been split apart and only half of it is left.

Looking at it makes me feel sick. Something warm is trickling down the side of my face. I rub it with my sleeve, and find that it is blood.

People are crowding round, talking and making sympathetic noises. This is very embarrassing.

I must get to my feet.

Hands are under my elbows, helping. I manage to struggle up.

I feel dizzy. My head hurts a lot.

The young man who has helped me up is frowning in concern. Curly brown hair covers his forehead, reaching the collar of his coat. A Royalist.

A woman says to him, "You'd best get your wife home, son. And your little lad as well."

He doesn't bother to tell her I am not his wife, just says, "Yes."

Jeffrey stares up at her, then at me, and notices the blood

on my face. He clings to my skirt and bursts into tears all over again.

A man puts a dented milk churn beside me and says, "I think this is yours."

Yes. I was going to get milk. It seems a long time ago.

"I'll carry that," says the young man, then asks me, "Where do you live?"

I can't seem to explain. Words are not working very well.

"She's Arthur Pomfret's daughter," the man who found the churns says. "The saddler. Out along the Burgate road."

"Right."

He puts his hand under my arm and asks, "Can you walk, do you think?"

"Yes," I say, though I am not sure.

We set out. Jeffrey is clinging to my free hand, still grizzling about his damaged puppet.

It is less than a mile, but it seems a long way. Every time I close my eyes I feel as if I am going to fall down.

Here is the house. I stop. Papa must not see me with a Royalist.

"You've been very kind," I tell him, "but I can manage now."

"I'll get the milk for you," he says. "Do you want the churn full or just half?"

"Full, please."

I'm fishing in my skirt pocket. The coins are still there. I put them in his hand.

He looks at them. Then he looks at me and says, "Tell me your name."

"Hannah Pomfret."

"I'm Matthew Wainwright. I'll leave the churn outside your door. I'd better not come into the house."

I know what he means. He is a Royalist and my father's views are well known.

We search each other's faces for a long moment. He has grey eyes, very steady.

"Will you be all right?" he asks.

"Yes. Thank you."

He steps back a couple of paces, still looking at me. Then he turns and walks away, the milk churn dangling from his hand.

DIFFERENCES

We are sitting by the fire, Mama, Elizabeth and me, mending clothes. It is a never-ending task. Boys seem unable to walk past any thorn bush without catching a sleeve and tearing it, and the knees are out of their breeches almost before the last patch has been sewn on. But though my fingers are busy with stitching and darning, my mind runs free. I am back again in yesterday's strange, dizzy morning, walking home with pain throbbing in my head and a strong hand under my arm.

Matthew Wainwright.

Matthew Wainwright.

His name repeats itself again and again like a tune that is stuck in the mind. But it is not clear like music, it fills me with confusion. His beliefs are the ones my father hates. He is a supporter of King Charles, an enemy of the true Presbyterian religion. A Cavalier, not a Roundhead. And yet…

When the hands are busy, the mind is free to remember. I am back in a hot August day four years ago, when I was only ten. Mama and I are in the market. A squad of Roundhead soldiers marches in with axes and battering rams as well as guns. They go in through the great front door of the Cathedral, and a sound of crashing and splintering begins. Everyone runs to see what is happening, but guards block the way. A woman says, "They are smashing everything." People are shaking their fists at us and I don't understand why. Mama says, "Hannah, come away." We turn to go but a man shouts in our faces, "Your soldiers are barbarians." And I know for the first time that our plain grey clothes marked us out as Puritans.

Thinking of it now, I remember that when we got home, Mama sat down and wept. I had never seen her cry before, and I thought she must be ill. I was frightened and asked if I should fetch Papa, but she shook her head quickly and said, "No, no, he would be angry. I must not be upset."

We had bought a length of grey linen to make me a new dress. I still wear it for housework, though it is tight across my chest now and shows my ankles. Every time I put it on, I think of that day. Michael came home with a cut lip because he and Will had been in a fight with some Royalist boys on the way back from school. James said the Protestant soldiers had found a store of arms in the Cathedral, and barrels of gunpowder, so the Cathedral elders must have been in a plot against the Parliament.

I'll never know if that was true – but the soldiers ripped up the paintings with their bayonets anyway, and smashed the carved pews. The gunfire we'd heard was from dozens of shots that destroyed the white marble statue of Christ. Papa said they acted correctly, but I was secretly grieved.

The Dean was imprisoned for secreting arms and explosives in the Cathedral, but they let him out when the King and Queen came to Canterbury. The pews were quickly mended for the royal visit and there was a fresh embroidered cloth on the communion table.

I finish the patch I had been stitching on Will's breeches, and thread a broader needle with wool to darn a hole in one of Papa's stockings.

My mind runs back to old memories like a disobedient dog. A man who came to collect a saddle from my father was full of news about a new attack on the Cathedral. I was hanging up washing outside the workshop and overheard his gleeful words.

"Blue Dick – what a man! He grabbed a pike from a soldier, hitched up his gown and was up that ladder quick as a squirrel, smashing the coloured glass out of the windows like a mad thing."

Blue Dick was the Rev. Richard Culmer, who always wore a blue habit.

My needle goes in and out steadily, weaving a cross-thread through the hole-spanning stitches I have put from side to side.

I still grieve for the lovely colours of the stained glass, but loving such things is a sin.

I still think of Matthew Wainwright and his steady grey eyes.

That is even more sinful, but I cannot stop.

A dreadful thing has happened. Mama has lost the baby she was expecting. He was born late one night – very quickly. Papa woke James and told him to run for the midwife, but by the time she came panting in, I was blowing desperately into the tiny baby's mouth and trying to get his little lungs to take a first breath. The midwife took him from me, then shook her head. "He has been born too early," she said. "Look at him, dear – he weighs no more than a little rabbit."

We buried him outside the wall of the Presbyterian churchyard, where babies lie who have not been baptized. Mama called him Peter, but he has no engraved headstone. His elder sister, who died before I was born, had been properly baptized and named, so she has a small stone in the churchyard. *Margaret Ann Pomfret Aged Seven Months.*

Mama was too ill to come to the funeral. We were afraid she had the childbed fever that kills so many women, but after about ten days of bathing her and giving her boiled water, she knew us again. I am looking after her and feeding her with chicken broth and custards and junket, but she is exhausted and cannot get out of bed. Elizabeth is helping as best she can. We do the washing between us, and prepare meals for Papa and the children. James does the marketing in the town. He is very strong and carries as much on his own as Mama and I can manage between us. Sometimes he buys the wrong things, but we do not complain. At morning prayers, Papa gives thanks that Mama is still alive. Amen to that. Oh, dear Lord, Amen.

I'm hoeing turnips in the garden, careful that the blade takes out weeds but does not cut through the roots of young plants.

A clopping of hooves stops at the gate. It's a heavy draught-horse, in full harness but pulling no cart. A man is astride it with the long driving reins bundled in his hands. He jumps down and loops the reins over the fence then opens the gate.

My heart almost stops.

It can't be. This is a dream. But he has seen me, and he stops at the workshop door to raise a hand.

Matthew Wainwright.

He goes to the workshop door. He is holding a long leather strap with a ragged end.

"I'm sorry to bother you," I hear him say to Papa, "but I've a broken trace."

Papa says, "You'll be wanting it right away, I suppose."

"If you can. I left a cartload of thatching reeds on the road. My father is waiting for them."

"I'll make you a new one. It shouldn't take long. There's a bench by the back door, you can wait there."

"Thank you."

He walks to the bench, but he does not sit down. His eyes are on mine, and he comes to the garden.

I can find no words. Neither can he, it seems. We just stand and stare at each other. We are both smiling.

He asks, "Are you better now?"

"Yes. You were very kind."

What can I do to be of service to him?

"Are you thirsty?" I ask. "Would you like some water?"

"Thank you," he says. "That would be welcome."

He comes with me to the well. I let the bucket down then start turning the handle to wind it up again, but he says, "I'll do that."

He winds the heavy bucket more quickly than I can. I fetch a jug and two mugs from the kitchen, and we fill them and take them back to the garden. We sit on the grass under the apple tree that is starting to set small fruit.

"I was lucky the trace broke so near to here," Matthew says.

"Yes."

He glances at the workshop door.

"I wanted to see you again but – it was difficult."

"Yes," I say again. The minutes are so precious, and they are running away so fast.

I blurt out, "I wish things were different."

He turns to me eagerly. "Do you? Do you really?"

"Yes. Really. But…"

His smile fades.

"I know. Your father did not want to talk to me just now, but I am a customer and he knows my father. I don't want to be his enemy. I did not choose to be born into a Royalist family. None of us can choose. You find yourself where you are."

If anywhere.

I think of the tiny baby that could not choose to live. Matthew and I are lucky. But all the same…

"If you could have chosen," I ask him, "would you still be a Royalist?"

"Yes."

But he frowns, trying to explain.

"I don't believe the King can do no wrong. Neither do my parents. But I think they are right to praise and celebrate the world God made. Forgive me, I know this is not your belief. It's just that He gave us the skill to make pictures and carvings and music, and I feel we must use it."

What I am going to say to him may mean eternal damnation.

"So do I."

No bolt from heaven strikes me dead. The birds go on singing. Sunshine still flickers through the leaves of the apple tree.

"Do you? Do you really?" He seems excited.

"Yes. I mean – the stained-glass windows in the cathedral were so beautiful. The blue and crimson and purple. But

38

Papa says enjoying such things is self-indulgence. Perhaps he is right."

"Nobody can be sure. I was taught that we are here on the earth as witnesses. The animals and plants are part of God's world but they cannot stand aside from it and say, 'Look – how wonderful.' So God made human beings, to look and hear and find ways to show that we see it as wonderful."

"Oh!" It is such a lovely idea that the breath goes out of me in a sigh of pleasure.

"I want to be a musician," Matthew goes on. "Thatching is a good trade, I know that. My father expects that I will work with him. I am the only son, you see, though I have two sisters. But I want to do more detailed things."

"Do you play an instrument?"

"Yes – lute and harpsichord. But I'd like to know how to make them. And I want to write music that other people can sing and play." He shakes his head and laughs. "Why am I telling you all this?"

"Because I want to know."

I may never see him again. I must remember his smile, his grey eyes, the urgency of what he is saying.

"King Charles is not a good king, I admit that," he goes on, reckless now. "He has made some stupid mistakes, like trying to force his new prayer book on the Scots. But a faulty man who has inspired beliefs is better than tight-mouthed Cromwell and his pious austerity."

He frowns down at his strong hands, and I have a sudden sense of alarm. What is he going to tell me? He meets my eyes and takes a breath.

"Hannah – you will have to know this. I am going to join the Royalist army."

My hands fly to my mouth. "Oh, no!"

"My father does not approve. He says I serve God better by thatching houses than I can do on the battlefield. But thatching does nothing to oppose Cromwell."

Men have to have their great ideas, my mother said once when I was asking her why there had been war in England.

Papa comes out of the workshop. He glances at the empty bench, then sees us in the garden. His face is dark with anger as he approaches.

"Hannah, get on with your work," he orders.

I've already snatched up the hoe. I start chopping at the turnip row again.

Matthew runs to meet him, thanking him politely, handing over coins. He goes to the gate with the new trace, puts his foot on a crossbar then vaults onto the big carthorse, gathers up its long driving reins and kicks its flank. He is riding away. I watch, but he does not look back.

Papa comes across to me in the garden. He is still angry.

"What were you thinking of? That young man is about to join the King's army and fight against us. His own father told me. He himself thinks it is foolish."

"He was thirsty, Papa. I gave him some water."

My father picks up the two mugs from the grass and frowns down at them. Then he says, "There are things you need to understand. Come and sit down."

He leads the way to the well and refills the mugs from the jug I left there. I sit beside him on the bench.

He says, "We on the Protestant side face a hard task – harder, perhaps, than you realize. The man leading us is a brilliant soldier, but he has his shortcomings."

"Oliver Cromwell?"

"Yes. Many of the soldiers he commanded in the last war have not been paid, and they want their money. Cromwell is ignoring them, so they have appointed representatives called Agitators, to argue their case. I belong to a group called the Levellers, who support the soldiers. Our fight is not merely against an outmoded religion, Hannah. We must build justice in our country. Every man should be able to vote – not just the rich and powerful. The Royalists think quite differently. They have no interest in enabling common people to take part in the process of government. Do you understand?"

I am touched by his honest words.

"Yes, Papa. I do understand."

A thought occurs.

"Are you called Levellers because everyone should be on the same level?"

My father permits himself a small smile.

"Not quite. The Royalists gave us the name, and meant it as an insult. Levellers were rough, unskilled hedge-cutters. But we saw the wider meaning and adopted it gladly."

"Yes, of course. People should have the same rights."

He looks at me with fresh interest.

"It's a pity you were not born a boy, Hannah. You have a good intelligence. And young Wainwright, though wrong-headed, is correct to think we are at war again. The King has invited the Scots to invade England, as we feared. Battle is raging in the north."

I stare down at my hands clasped round my mug of water. It may be the one Matthew drank from. This could be the last connection between us. He is going to fight. He may be killed. But I can never think of him as an enemy.

A POEM AND A PRESENT

I am in the market on my own. So much has changed since that Christmas Day when I watched looting and fire-raising in the dreadful knowledge that I should not be here. I do the shopping now, and Mama stays at home. She is still weak from her illness after the lost baby, and I think she takes comfort from being with Jeffrey and Leah – especially Leah, who is not much more than a year old.

Among the crowds, I scan the faces of strangers, hoping to see Matthew, but weeks have gone by and I never do. My longing to be with him feels like a kind of illness. There is a constant heavy ache in my chest and I have no appetite. I help to prepare food and set it on the table, but trying to eat it seems too much effort. Mama worries and says I am getting thin, but I can't explain.

Oh! I catch a glimpse of a young man with curly brown hair and my heart leaps – but he turns his head and I see he is a stranger. *Walk on. Feel the weight of the shopping basket. Stop hoping.*

A sheet of paper with lines of verse printed on it blows past in the wind. There are copies of it all over the place, pinned on barrels and glued in shop windows, or muddied and trodden underfoot. I have not bothered to read what it says. But a group of Royalists are standing round a sheet that's nailed to a house door, and they seem excited. One of them shakes a fist in the air and says exultantly, "Yes!"

When they have gone, I make my way to the door, curious to see what they found so interesting. It will be some political tract, I expect, or a petition – but as I get closer, I can see that the lines are short, with gaps between sections like a hymn. I start to read. It is not a hymn, but a poem, called "To Althea from Prison", by a man called Richard Lovelace.

I read the words slowly, and am moved almost to tears. Richard dreams as I do of someone he loves. He is a Royalist, and he is writing from a prison cell, but I envy him… Although he is locked up, he is more fortunate than I am, because Althea, his true love, comes to the grating of his cell every night, and whispers to him and slips her hand through the bars to touch him. I skip quickly through the lines that praise the King for his wisdom and majesty, but I read the words of the last verse again and again.

Stone walls do not a prison make,
Nor iron bars a cage;
Minds innocent and quiet take
That for an hermitage;
If I have freedom in my love
And in my soul am free,
Angels alone, that soar above,
Enjoy such liberty.

I leave the paper where it is for others to read, but look round me and pick up a copy that has been blown into a doorway and is not wet or dirty. I read it once again, then fold it carefully and put it in my pocket.

On the way home, the words repeat themselves again and again in my mind – but when I come to the gate where Matthew tied his big horse, fear creeps in. There is no safe hiding place in our small house. If one of my brothers should find the poem, he would show it to Papa. And then there would be trouble.

I take the paper from my pocket and unfold it, then tuck it between a big stone and a foxglove plant, where it could have been blown by the wind.

More weeks have gone past. I am in the town again. It is raining, and I have to hold my skirt up with one hand to keep it clear of the puddles. A group of men have set up a small table outside the rebuilt draper's shop that was burned in the riots, and I glance at them without much interest. They are holding up sheets of paper pinned on boards, and shouting, "Sign the petition! Bring back the King!" People are clustered round the table, some to sign, others to object and argue.

One of the Royalists turns to speak to a man – and it is Matthew.

I approach slowly, hardly able to believe what I am seeing. Maybe I am mistaken. But he breaks off from wrangling with the man and comes to join me.

"Hannah!"

His hands are outstretched and he is smiling. For a dizzy moment, I think he is going to kiss me. He does not, of course, just clasps my arms above the elbows, and my more sensible mind is grateful. No nice Puritan girl could dream of kissing a man in public – particularly a Royalist with brown hair curling over his collar.

I say, "I thought you were in the army."

"I was. I did the basic training, but came back to help my father. Summer is a busy time, with reeds to cut and roofs to do while the weather holds. But have you heard the news?" He rushes on, "The Royalist prisoners have been found Not Guilty! They have all been pardoned and set free!"

"Richard Lovelace as well?"

"Yes, Richard, too." Then he looks surprised. "Do you know him?"

"No – but I read his poem."

"Isn't it wonderful? *If I have freedom in my love—*"

I join him.

"*And in my soul am free—*"

We speak the words together, careless of what people think.

"Hey, Matt!" one of his friends shouts. "Never mind the poetry – get her to sign the petition!"

The sheets of paper have dozens of names on them. Hundreds, perhaps. Even thousands, if people in other towns are doing this. At the top of each sheet, heavy printed letters shout their message.

We, the undersigned, demand the return to power of England's rightful monarch, King Charles.

The man who shouted to Matthew comes to join us.

"This scoundrel is Roger Blackburn," Matthew says. "Roger, this is Hannah Pomfret." The scoundrel has a dark beard and laughing eyes, and he shakes my hand.

"It's good to meet you, Hannah," he says. "Matt has told me so much about you."

What has he said?

I can't ask. Roger is offering me a pen, and his smile is slightly mocking now.

"I don't suppose you'll add your name."

"I'm sorry. Our family is … I mean…"

"Yes, of course."

He turns away, addressing a fresh bystander.

"How about you, sir?"

My face has reddened. I feel dreadful although I know what he asks is impossible.

"It's all right," Matthew says. "I know you can't."

A woman with several children and a large dog comes up and asks, "What's all this about, then?"

Probably she cannot read, let alone sign.

Matthew turns to her and starts explaining.

I hesitate for a few moments, but realize this has nothing to do with me, so I walk away. When I look back, Matthew is still talking to the woman. He has not noticed that I've gone.

James has just come in, looking triumphant.

"That's put paid to their petition," he says. "The Parliament has said it will hang two men from every parish if this goes on. Quite right, too."

Papa nods agreement. "It should have been done earlier," he says, "before this foolishness took hold. As things are now, I fear it may be too late. We may have to contend with organized rebellion." "Just let them try it," James says, making a gesture of pushing up first one sleeve then the other. "Two can play at that game."

I think of Matthew and Roger in the market three days

ago, with such high hopes that they could change everything. And of the Lovelace poem, rain-soaked now in its hidden place by the gate, slowly becoming part of the earth under the leaves of the foxglove plant.

There is nothing I can say.

Elizabeth, leaning on her crutch as always, comes out to the garden, where I am pulling young carrots to thin the rows. In her free hand, she is carefully carrying something wrapped in a white cloth. I go to meet her. She is so pretty, my sweet, lopsided sister. Her tidily pinned-up hair is fairer than mine, but she has dark-brown eyes, unexpected in her pale face.

She glances round to make sure we are alone then says quietly, "Hannah, he was outside, waiting in the lane. I went to the gate, but he wouldn't come in. He gave me this for you."

She puts the wrapped thing in my hands. It seems to weigh nothing. I open the white folds carefully. Inside is an intricately woven and twisted knot of wheat straw, tied at its top with a red ribbon. A corn dolly.

Elizabeth looks at it as well, then meets my eyes. "It is a love knot," she says.

"Yes."

I look at it again. A love knot. A keepsake.

A farewell.

The sun blurs with tears.

Elizabeth puts her arm round me, and holds me close.

"Dear, Hannah. I am so sorry."

She knows everything, and always has done. Why hadn't I realized? In her quiet hobbling round the house and in her unnoticed place by the fire, she has watched what goes on and understood. Now, her dark eyes are steady on my face.

"He asked me to give you a message. He is going to Maidstone, he said. He will be thinking of you."

"Maidstone?"

I am puzzled. I know nothing about Maidstone, except it is the County Town of Kent.

But Elizabeth knows.

"There is going to be a battle there. I heard Papa talking to some men who came to see him. The Royalists hold Maidstone, but the Parliamentary forces are determined to get them out. They plan to attack very soon – probably next week. So Royalist supporters are coming from everywhere to help defend it."

Matthew will be with them.

Elizabeth is watching me in concern.

"The war has come to us, Hannah," she says. "We must meet it as best we can."

"Yes."

She is right. And the best I can do is pray.

We go into the house. James comes in from the workshop, bursting with the news. I am so glad I already know about it – I will not be as shocked as he probably hoped.

"The Royalists think the New Model Army can't dislodge them from Maidstone," he says. "They know Cromwell and half his troops are away in Wales, dealing with a rebellion there, so his army is split. So the stupid idiots are grabbing the chance to try to take Dover – and Gravesend and Rochester, too – as well as hold Maidstone. If they do that, it leaves no more than two thousand men to defend Maidstone. What fools they are! We'll wipe them out."

He was terribly right. Yesterday, June 1st, Sir Thomas Fairfax led six thousand men into battle. He cleverly split his attack, James said, sending half his men across the river to raid the town from the far side as well. He had the Royalist troops pinned in Maidstone "like rats in a trap", James said, and went into gleeful detail.

"The fighting went on all day, in pouring rain that turned into a raging thunderstorm. So just after midnight, the Royalists gave in. There were heavy casualties, but our side had very few losses."

I pray constantly that Matthew is unharmed, though I know Papa would say such prayers are a sinful wish to oppose God's will.

I don't know what I can do. I am lost.

Three days have gone by. I do not know if Matthew is dead

or alive. Nobody can help me. There is only one thing to do.

I am standing on the doorstep of Matthew's house. I raise the heavy knocker on the door, and let it fall lightly, but it makes a much louder bang than I intended.

A man with curly grey hair opens it. He must be Matthew's father, they are so alike. He gives me an enquiring smile that is not frightening, but I have to clear my throat before I can speak.

"I'm sorry to disturb you, but it's just – I wondered – is there any news of Matthew? I mean, after Maidstone?"

It sounds terribly muddled. He looks at me with new interest.

"You'll be the girl he has been mooning over," he says. "Arthur Pomfret's daughter, if I'm not mistaken. Hannah, is it?"

"Yes."

"Come along in."

I follow him into the front room. He pulls out a chair beside a big, polished table, and says, "Do sit down."

"Well, Hannah," he goes on, "you've chosen a difficult path."

"I know."

My mind is running about like a frightened rabbit. Matthew must be dead. His father is trying to find a way to tell me. I'm fighting back tears but I must try to sound sensible.

"I did not mean to choose it."

"We none of us get a choice," he says. "But the news is

good. Matthew is alive and uninjured."

The breath goes out of me in relief.

"Oh – thank God."

His father goes on, "Like you, my wife and I were desperately anxious. We'd hoped he would return home after the battle, but there was no sign of him. We didn't know what had happened until he arrived here yesterday. He'd sensibly hidden in a ditch until Cromwell's soldiers had gone. Then he walked home. He only dared move at night for safety, so it took some time."

He frowns. "But I'm afraid this is not the end of it, Hannah. He is even more determined to fight for the King. There is to be another battle quite soon, here in Canterbury."

"In *Canterbury*?"

I have seen what can happen when beliefs clash, but armed, official warfare will be far worse. Countless people will be killed. And I do not believe the Royalists can win. James said before Maidstone, "They haven't a chance. Cromwell's army has thousands of well-trained men." He was right. And I fear he will be right again. I am plunged back into dismay.

"I know what you are thinking," Mr Wainwright says, "and I share it. Do we really have to go through this awful anxiety again, so soon? But Matthew sees it as his duty. I blame myself a little. Perhaps my wife and I made our beliefs too clear. It never occurred to us that our son might answer a call to arms – but he is young, and young men believe in their own strength, and their ability to improve the world. They cannot bear to stand aside and be thought cowards."

He looks at me in fresh concern.

"Do your parents know how you feel about Matthew?"

I shake my head, and he sighs.

"Your father and I know each other quite well, of course," he goes on. "As leading tradesmen in Canterbury, we have concerns in common. And we are civilized men. We can accept our differences."

"Oh, but please—"

I'm terrified that he means to tell Papa about my visit.

He smiles. "Don't look so frightened," he says. "I will respect your confidence. I have no wish to make trouble for you, or for my son. There are bigger things to worry about."

He surveys me without hurry, the grey eyes, so like his son's, travelling across my face. He says, "You seem a thoughtful girl, Hannah. If things were different, you would make a good wife for my son. But we are at war again, and whether we like it or not, sides have to be taken. Very few of us can say we are neutral. It is going to be hard for you. Hard for all of us."

"Yes."

Part of my mind is thinking that Matthew must be in

the house somewhere. I wish his father would offer to fetch him, or at least tell I am here, but he does not. Perhaps, after a week of fighting and walking, probably with little food or sleep, he may still be in his bed.

Mr Wainwright stands up. I do, too.

"I am sure we will meet again," he says, extending a hand to shake. "Let us hope it will be in happier circumstances."

WAR IN CANTERBURY

Papa gave strict instructions that we were to stay in the house, though James was in the thick of it. He came back unharmed except for a ripped sleeve and a cut across the back of his hand. And he could not wait to tell us what had happened.

I do not want to remember the details of what he said. The hideous deaths and heroic daring that excited him so much seemed horrible to me – and to Elizabeth as well. We did not look at each other while he was speaking, but in bed that night, we admitted that we were glad the forces had been so unequal. At least it meant the fighting was over more quickly.

We'd seen the Parliamentary army marching across the meadows that surround our house. There seemed thousands of them, a grey tide of helmeted men marching with their pikes and muskets in parallel slanting lines. James, who had gone with them as a volunteer, along with a good number of local boys, said there were at least seven thousand, and he thought it might have been nearer eight, so the hopes of a split and reduced army were all wrong. And there were only thirteen hundred Royalists trying to hold Canterbury.

"We are in control of the city now," James boasted. "And we will stay in control."

The Parliamentary soldiers had torn the city gates off their hinges and burned them, he said. "And then we took the guns and other weapons from the beaten soldiers and stored the whole lot in the Cathedral. And guess what?" he went on. "Cromwell ordered the cavalry to stable its horses in there – three hundred of them! What price their holy sculptures now? Their precious Cathedral is no more than a barn, full of captured guns and horse shit."

Elizabeth and I dared not look at each other.

I have been back to Matthew's house. His father had no news of him, but he thought he would have heard if Matthew had been killed. It was more likely that he had stayed with what remained of the Royalist army.

James says the few Royalist army survivors went north to London, but found the city gates barred against them. "So most of them deserted," he added, "cowards that they are." The rest, it seems, are making their way to a place called Chelmsford, in Essex, to join with what he called "rabble of their own kind".

Perhaps Matthew is with them. Dear Lord, if he is alive, take care of him.

The nights are full of terrible dreams, and I wake in such panic that I am scared to go back to sleep again. Elizabeth wakes sometimes as well and does her best to comfort me, but I try not to disturb her.

Mama said this morning, "Hannah, you don't look at all well these days. I am worried about you."

I told her I had caught a chill, but I don't think she believed me.

Papa calls me as I pass his workshop door.

"Hannah – come here for a minute."

He is at his bench, stamping buckle-holes into a bridle strap. He puts the leather down and turns to face me. He does not look angry.

"Your mother is concerned about you," he says. "And so am I. What is troubling you, child?"

Mama will have passed on my tale about catching a chill, but he has not believed it. I have to tell him something like the truth.

"It seems so terrible, Papa."

"What does?"

"This war."

He looks at me carefully.

"Do you understand why the war has to be fought?" he asks.

"Because the Parliament is right and the King is wrong."

I sound tired, and of course he is not satisfied.

"In what way is the King wrong?"

"Lots of ways."

I don't want to go over it all again, but he is waiting for more.

"The Queen is a Catholic," I offer, but he brushes that aside.

"The Queen has been in France for several years," he says. "Our quarrel is not with her. It is with King Charles, who signed a treaty with the Scots, inviting them to invade our country, thus committing an act of treachery. Can we accept a traitor as our king?"

"No, Papa."

"Then – you can see this war is necessary."

"Yes, Papa."

"So why do you find it terrible?"

What can I say?

"It's just – so many men are being killed. Fathers who have children. Young men who – who have – people who care for them."

My voice cracks and I swallow hard. My father is looking at me with suspicion and concern.

"Hannah," he says, surprisingly gently. "Your mother thinks you have fallen in love. Is that true?"

Tears overflow. I duck away from him and run out of the workshop, across the yard, through the garden and out over the field, until my trembling legs bring me to the edge of the forest. And there, I lean my head against the smooth grey bark of a beech tree, and cry and cry.

I sit on my parents' bed, rocking Leah's cradle gently with my foot to lull her to sleep. She is getting too big for the cradle now, and lies with her knees drawn up, but Mama seems in no hurry to move her into the same bed as Jeffrey, who sleeps in James's attic room upstairs. She told me the other day that she will have no more children. "I have become an old woman," she said. "Perhaps it is a good thing."

I do not think of her as old. If anything, she has seemed younger and stronger since she recovered from the loss of the baby. She is in the small room above this one at the moment, telling Will and Michael to blow their candle out. She asked me to wait here for her. After I ran away from Papa's questioning, I know what she will ask.

Here she is. She sits down on the chair by the small window. Leah is asleep, so I stop rocking the cradle. It is dark in here, but a half moon rides in the sky and I can see the pale shape of Mama's face. She leans forward and puts her hand over mine.

"Hannah," she says. "Please tell me. Who is it?"

We can't be heard from downstairs, but I am frozen with caution.

"You don't have to worry, Mama."

"Yes, I do. My dear, I know what you are going through. You see – I have never told anyone this, but – your father was not my first love."

I'm astonished. I had always assumed that my meek,

obedient mother had married Papa when she was young and never dreamed of anyone else.

She sits back.

"I loved a boy called Daniel," she goes on. "We used to meet in secret, though it was difficult. But his parents were rich and they'd arranged that he would marry the daughter of rich friends. When they found out we were meeting, they forbade him to see me again. So that was the end of it."

"You mean, he *agreed*?" I am appalled. "That's dreadful!"

"It was hard for him," she says. "A hard choice. As it is for you."

She reaches for my hand again and rubs her thumb gently over the back of it.

"Tell me who your friend is, Hannah. I'll do my best to help you."

But she will tell my father.

"He is a Royalist, isn't he?" she persists.

"Yes." I can't tell her a straight lie.

"When did it begin?"

"It was that day…"

I can't go on. But it is enough. She knows.

"When you got knocked down?"

"Yes."

She nods. "It's the boy who helped you home, isn't it?"

How does she know? Matthew did not come in.

"Jeffrey talked about him," she goes on. "He thought he was very nice. Matthew Wainwright?"

"Yes."

There. It has been said.

"I thought so," Mama says. "When your father told me you were talking to him in the garden, I knew what must have happened."

So simple, I suppose. So obvious. But now I'm terrified.

"Please don't tell Papa! *Please*!"

"My dear, I have to tell him. It will be much worse if he hears about it through gossip. And gossip is bound to start sooner or later. Your father loves you, Hannah. You must remember that."

"He loves God more."

Mama gives a little gasp, and I start a stumbling apology.

"I'm sorry, I should not have said – I mean, the love of God must come first, I know that. It's just…"

Just that so many thousands have died for the love of their God. Not just martyrs and soldiers, but innocent people who get caught up in wars through no fault of their own.

Mama sighs.

"I sometimes think women are different," she says. "In their minds, I mean. Children are born because a man has fathered them, but God sends that life – or takes it away. There is no point in looking for a reason. In the end, it is the same for all of us."

I think of Margaret, the elder sister I never knew, who is buried under the stone with her name on it. And of little Peter, who lies in an unmarked grave outside the church wall. Surely he, too, must be with God, who sent his life and so quickly took it away?

Mama says, "Please don't tell your father what I said. I would hate to hurt him.'"

"Of course not."

I stare at her in a mixture of admiration and sadness.

She is so brave, and so kind. She would never hurt anyone. But she will betray me.

We kneel in prayer in the front room.

"Oh Lord our Governor," Papa says, eyes closed over his joined hands, "if it be Your will, send guidance to Hannah, who has strayed from the true course of Your ways. We acknowledge that as sinful humans we do deserve no mercy, but we beg You to forgive her. Bring her again, we pray, into the infinite compassion of Your love, and help her to see the folly and wickedness of following her own will. In the name of Jesus Christ, our Lord, Amen."

"Amen," I whisper with the others.

The younger ones are glancing at me over their hands, not understanding what it is about. James and Mama still have their eyes closed. Elizabeth's head is bowed, and nobody can see her face.

Papa gets to his feet. "We will begin our day's work," he says, then adds, "Hannah, you will remain here."

A babble of talk bursts out as soon as they have left the room, but it is hushed quickly by my mother.

"James, shut the door," Papa calls, and it closes.

"Sit down, Hannah."

I sit on one of the hard-backed chairs, but he remains standing. He stares at me as though I had become an incomprehensible thing. When he speaks, his voice has lost the entreaty of his prayer. It is stiff with displeasure.

"The injury you do to me and to your family is nothing compared with the sin you are committing in the sight of God. Do you realize that?"

Until now I have managed not to cry, but his harsh words make my heart feel constricted and my throat aches with tears. I cannot answer.

"The Lord made us responsible for our own actions," he continues, "and expects that we will accept that responsibility. Do you understand me, Hannah?"

"Yes, Papa."

"In that case, there is no more to be said. You will of course repent your sin and seek the forgiveness of God and of those you have injured."

He takes a step closer.

"But understand this. I will hear no more of this person with whom you are infatuated. You will not see him again.

You understand me?"

"Yes, Papa."

I understand him very well. It is what I expected.

I wipe my eyes in weariness and wish I could be away in the quiet woods where no human voice speaks any words.

"Come here, my child," he says more kindly.

I stand up and approach him.

He takes both my hands, as Mama did, though his palms are harder and rougher than hers.

"You are not alone, Hannah," he says. "All of us go through these temptations. It is part of God's way to test us and make us strong."

"Yes, Papa."

He is waiting for me to say I am sorry. But if I deny my love for Matthew, God will know I am lying.

He sighs and says, "Let us pray together."

We kneel.

It seems the end of everything.

NEWS

Weeks have gone past, blank and empty. It is the end of August, almost autumn now. I have thought of going to Matthew's house, but what good would it do? Somebody might see me and tell Papa and things would be even worse. My hopes are almost dead. I buy a rabbit at the butcher's stall. I don't like skinning them, but they are cheap and make a good pie.

Someone touches my shoulder. I turn, and for a moment, my heart leaps. It is Roger Blackburn, who was collecting signatures for their petition. But he is alone, and his bearded face is grave.

"Hannah – I was hoping I'd see you."

I hold my breath in terror of what he is going to say.

"It's all right," he reassures me quickly, "Matthew is alive. But have you heard about Colchester?"

"No."

James and Papa never mention the war in front of me now.

"Where is Colchester?"

"In Essex. Matt and I ended up there after the Maidstone

battle. We only meant to go to London, but the gates were shut. Our commander had news that the rebellion in Essex was still going strong, so we crossed the river and went on up to Chelmsford. But the people we met there said we were needed in Colchester, which is further north. The Royalists still held the town, but Parliamentary forces had surrounded it. And they meant business. They had over five thousand men, and a thousand cavalry. Friends managed to smuggle us into the town on a dark night, and the next day we fought the Parliamentary men off and thought we had won. But they sealed the gates and put the town under siege. No traffic could get in or out. Supplies were cut off and there was no food. People were starving. They ate their horses. They even ate dogs and cats, but the children were dying – everyone was dying. We were starving, too, though we'd commandeered food from the townspeople when we first arrived. I feel ashamed to think of that now. Half-dead women went to the gates to beg the Parliamentary commander for food, and he let them out – but then gave his soldiers permission to strip them naked and do with them as they chose."

All this is terrible, but I am desperate to know about Matthew.

Roger goes on, "We broke out the next night and tried to ride for help. Matthew was with us. A thousand of us got as far as a place called Boxted, but we ran into a massive ambush. They opened fire and mowed us down. Matt was shot through the shoulder. We managed to get him away, but there was no hope of taking him with us on the retreat south. His shoulder was a mess, and he'd lost a lot of blood. He couldn't walk, let alone ride. Some local people said they'd take care of him. Royalist supporters, good folk. They promised to write and tell me if – if anything happened. But I've not heard from them."

Roger looks at me in concern.

"Are you all right? You've gone very pale."

I feel dizzy and in need of something to hold on to, and it's hard to make my voice sound steady.

"How will you know what's happened? Will they – can they – I mean..."

I take a breath and ask what I really want to know.

"Will he come back?"

"I don't know," Roger says. "I hope so. He's young and strong; he's got every chance. But we didn't have much time, you see. We needed to get away. It was all very confused."

"Yes. Yes, of course."

I must not look on the dark side, it does no good. But wounds go septic, gangrene can set in. There's a request I must make.

"Roger – promise you'll tell me if you hear anything. Even if it's bad news. I'd rather know than wait and wonder forever."

"Of course I will. But – I'd better not come to your house. Your father—"

"I won't care what my father says. If it's good news, it won't matter. And if it's bad…"

I can't go on.

If Matthew dies, nothing will matter ever again.

Elizabeth watches me constantly, doing little kindnesses whenever she can. She is the only person who knows what Roger told me. In our whispered conversations in bed at night, she says I must keep up my hopes. No news is good news, she insists.

Mama worries about me, I can see that. She does not know what has happened, but she wishes she could help.

Nobody can help.

There has been another battle, this time at a place in the north of England called Preston. James says it is the last. The Royalists lost so disastrously that the war is now over. Scottish Royalists had joined up with the English Cavaliers but Cromwell's Parliamentary troops, the body known as the New Model Army, were stronger and both better armed and better disciplined. And there were far more of them.

Papa gave thanks at prayers this morning for the final defeat of "the menace of Royalism". Elizabeth's eyes met mine over her joined hands, steady and reassuring. Two thousand Scottish and English Royalists were killed at Preston, and nine thousand taken prisoner, but Matthew could not have been among them. His earlier injury would have prevented that.

My enemy now is the everlasting silence. Hope is beginning to die.

A sound of hooves and cartwheels falls silent at the gate.

Mama is busy rubbing butter into flour for a second batch of scones. "Hannah, see who that is," she says.

I put down the stocking I am mending and go out. A sturdy cob pulling a trap has come to a halt. The driver is opening the gate.

It is John Wainwright. Dread sweeps over me like cold water. He has come to break bad news. But he looks across and raises a hand, smiling.

"I have brought you a surprise," he says.

He indicates a huddled figure on the seat of the trap. I look more closely, and gasp.

It is Matthew. But he is sitting hunched and sideways, the cob's reins held loosely in one hand. His other arm is in a sling, and the shoulder on that side looks shapeless and collapsed.

Our eyes meet, but his face is white and uncertain.

I want to run to him, but I seem paralysed. Elizabeth has followed me out, and she limps quickly to Matthew's father, hand extended in welcome. "Come in. Do please come in." She turns her head and calls, "Mama! Mama! We have visitors!"

Jeffrey comes running out, with Leah toddling behind him, followed by Mama, wiping her hands on a cloth.

"Oh, my goodness!" she says.

Matthew is climbing laboriously down from the trap, helped by his father.

James comes out of the workshop and stares. Without saying a word, he turns on his heel and goes back to fetch Papa.

Will and Michael are at school, thank goodness. They would have been full of tactless questions and comments. As it is, Matthew and his father make their slow way towards us while we stare in dread at the workshop door. I can't bear it, and look instead at a dandelion by my feet.

When Papa comes out, he shakes hands with Matthew's father as though they have just met casually in the town.

"Good to see you, John," he says. "You are welcome."

He turns his head and surveys Matthew without hurry, observing the useless arm supported by the white sling tied round his neck, then turns back to Mr Wainwright and says, "I am sorry to see that your son has been injured."

Mr Wainwright acknowledges this with a nod, and waits for more.

Papa goes on, but now there is an icy edge to his voice.

"My wife has given me to understand that there is a liking between your son and my daughter. Since you have come here, you force me to give my opinion."

He turns to me.

"As we have said before, Hannah, you are old enough to start thinking about becoming a man's wife. It is natural that you are in the grip of powerful feelings. But I have to say this. Setting aside the question of this young man's mistaken beliefs, I would expect you to have enough sense to pick a husband who can earn his living."

Elizabeth takes my hand in hers and grips it tightly. The silence is tense.

Papa returns his attention to Matthew's father and says, "I am sorry, John. But we are honest men. We must face the facts."

"So be it," says John Wainwright. "You have a right to your opinions."

He puts his hand under Matthew's undamaged arm and says, "Come along, Matthew. There is nothing more we can do here."

Papa and James go back to the workshop. Matthew and his father are leaving.

Mama is flustered and distraught. "Oh, please – don't go," she says. "I mean, you are very welcome. I've just made some fresh scones. Do come in. Please."

Matthew speaks for the first time.

"Thank you," he says. "But we should not trouble you any further."

He looks at me.

"Hannah, I had to let you see the way things are. It was only fair. But your father is right. I cannot do anything that needs two strong arms. I am no use to you."

Leah, unusually, for she is a shy child, runs across to him and takes his good hand.

"You coming in," she says.

With Jeffrey running and jumping as usual and Leah still holding Matthew's hand, we muddle our way into the kitchen. Elizabeth is there already, setting a jug of milk on the table, where she has put fresh-baked scones on a big plate, with butter and new raspberry jam.

"We'd have used the front room," Mama frets, "but I didn't know you were coming."

Matthew's father soothes her.

"Please don't think of it. We were not expecting to be invited in. And in our own home, we spend most of our time in the kitchen."

Remembering the cool front room where we sat down when I went to his house on that first day, I doubt if that is true. But I am grateful for his tact.

As John Wainwright talks easily to my mother, I can only look at Matthew. In these long weeks, I have constantly imagined seeing him again, but always thought it would be just the two of us, under trees perhaps, or in the long grass of an open meadow. But here we all are, mixed together in this familiar kitchen. I feel no more than a bystander.

Jeffrey is staring at Matthew with interest.

"What have you done to your arm?" he asks.

Mama tries to hush him, but Matthew smiles and says, "It's a reasonable question."

He tells Jeffrey, "I was in a war. I was wounded."

Jeffrey nods. "I was in a war, too. Ned's head got broken."

"I know," Matthew says, "I was there."

Jeffrey has run to fetch his rabbit puppet. With his hand inside it, he claps its paws happily and says, "Michael made him a new head."

"What a lucky rabbit," says Matthew. "I'm lucky, too. It's only my arm that got hurt. You can't make a new head for a human."

"Why not?" Jeffrey asks.

"That's enough," Mama tells him – but Matthew doesn't seem to mind.

"Ned's head is made of wood," he explains. "It's wood all the way through. But a human head has got a brain inside it."

"What's a brain?"

"It's what you think with."

"How do you—"

Elizabeth gives Jeffrey a scone and says, "Run and eat that outside so the birds can have the crumbs."

He does as she says.

Mama has poured mugs of home-brewed ale for Matthew and his father. I take Leah on my lap and help her drink a cup of milk. I can't seem to eat anything.

It seems no time before Matthew's father gets to his feet.

"You have been very kind," he tells Mama, "and the scones were delicious. But we must be getting back."

My own voice surprises me with its urgency.

"Oh, no—"

After these terrible weeks of waiting, I cannot bear to see him go away, as if there is nothing to be said.

We stare at each other across the table, and for a brief moment we seem alone together, though the room is full of people. He is getting to his feet, but he pauses.

"I would like to see Hannah again," he says to Mama. "Will that be possible?"

My mother is flustered all over again.

"It's not for me to say," she says, "I don't know what my husband—"

Elizabeth puts in two forceful, unexpected words.

"Mama! *Please!*"

It sends a shock through the air. The little ones look at her, as startled as though Jeffrey's rabbit had spoken.

Mama's face flushes.

"Well – I suppose – I mean, yes, of course, but I can't…"

She wants to be kind to me, but she does not dare.

"That's kind of you," says Matthew's father easily. "And I do understand how things are. But there's no hurry. We can take our time. Thank you very much for your hospitality."

We all shake hands. Matthew's good right hand feels warm and smooth as it always did. It is the first time I have touched him since that day when the cabman's horse bolted and he came from nowhere to help me.

At the gate, the tethered cob turns its head to watch Matthew being helped into the trap as if it is concerned for him.

Papa does not look at me now. Even if I get in his way in our crowded house, he does not so much as glance at me when I stand back to let him pass.

Mama, Elizabeth and I seem very separate from the others. Will and Michael are growing up fast, and they want to be like James, taking an interest in the events of the wider world outside our cottage and having opinions about them. We, the females, are not included in their discussions. Papa used to answer my questions and listen to my ideas, but all that has stopped. In his eyes, I have joined the enemy. I wish I could explain that Matthew and I do not think of each other as Royalist and Puritan. We are simply two people.

Or are we? In truth I know very little about Matthew. Perhaps he has become a soldier, for whom everyone is either a comrade or an enemy. I don't feel this can be true, but I have no way to prove or disprove it. I must see him. If he has begun to think like a soldier and has nothing to say to me any more, then it is better to know. And if he still cares for me, then I must be with him. So I will have to go and see him. At least I know his father will not mind.

I am fifteen now. Although I am useful to Mama, she will not expect me to spend the rest of my life here. She is stronger now and can manage better. I know she still grieves for the lost baby, but I am secretly glad she is not burdened with yet another child to feed and care for. Matthew is the one who needs help now. But that is easy to say. He may have changed. But whatever the truth, I must know.

RISK

This time I do not go to the front door, but follow the flint-edged path round to the back of the house. It leads to a paved yard with stables and a coach house. The wall opposite has an arch in it that spans a broad drive, leading out between meadows. Apart from a few pigeons pecking for spilled grain in the autumn sunshine, the yard is empty and silent. There is no sound of footsteps or voices. Rooks arguing in a stand of distant elm trees sound loud and clear. Further along the wall to my right, there is a porch with plants on its window ledge, some of them still bearing red flowers. I feel as furtive as a burglar, though I am not here to steal but to give. Very quietly, I edge along towards the porch and the door. But to get there, I have to pass a window.

For a stupid moment, I gather up my skirt, intending to creep past the pane bent double in case someone inside should see me, then scold myself. I am not a burglar. And somebody has to see me if there is to be any point to this visit.

I come to the window and turn my head to look in.

Matthew is sitting at a table. I have walked straight into his gaze.

"Hannah!" he says.

With his good arm, he pushes his chair back from the table. He jumps to his feet as quickly as he can, then hurries to the porch door. Here he is – in front of me. And I do not know what to say. We stand facing each other. He laughs, a little breathlessly.

"Hannah," he says again, "this is wonderful."

I'm babbling some kind of answer.

"When you came with your father – it was so difficult. I knew you could not visit us again."

His face is thinner, but his grey eyes are the same, steady and careful.

"It was difficult," he says. "I wanted so much to see you again, but it would have caused trouble if I came to your house." Then he laughs and says, "why are we standing here? Come in, come in."

He leads the way into the room where he was sitting. It is not the kitchen, which is on the other side of the back door, but a small study, lined with bookshelves. Papers are strewn on the table, and a pen stands in the inkwell.

"I was trying to write to you," he says. "I have been trying for days, but I can't find the words. Please, do sit down." He adds, "There's nobody here. My father is out at a cottage, doing a roof, and my mother has gone to the market. There is a servant, but she is upstairs. Making beds or something."

So I am alone with a Royalist soldier. Papa does not know where I am, but I feel his fury, and tremble a little. But my eyes do not leave Matthew's. There is so much to be said that it is like being hungry at a feast. We don't know where to start – or what will happen when we do.

I ask, "how are you?" and feel like my mother on a polite visit.

He doesn't think it's absurd.

"Getting better," he says. He indicates the sling. "I wear this because it's more comfortable if the arm is supported. But I'm getting stronger every day."

"That's good."

Silence enfolds us again. I wonder if he, too, feels guilty. His comrades and perhaps his family might well frown if they knew he was here alone with a Puritan girl. Whether I like it or not, my grey dress and demure white cap mark me as being on the side of the Parliamentary army that nearly killed him.

If this is in his mind, he brushes it away. He says, "I am supposed to walk every day. The doctor says exercise improves the circulation and makes the muscles work again. But walking alone is very tedious. If you have time, would you perhaps come with me?"

"Yes. I'd like to."

In fact, I'd be relieved. Being alone with him in this house makes me feel uneasy. The servant may come down from upstairs at any moment and be startled to find us here, then gossip about the disgraceful girl who came seeking the young master. If we are seen walking together outside, it could be a chance encounter, but a visit to a house cannot be accidental.

Matthew closes the back door quietly behind us, and we walk under the arch and follow the drive across the fields, then take the narrow path that slopes gently upward and leads to a beech wood. I worry a little that he may be finding the walk tiring, but his pace matches mine, and he does not seem out of breath. He glances at me and laughs.

"Don't look so anxious," he says. "I really am better. The main trouble was I'd lost such a lot of blood, and I was very weak. My mother has been feeding me good meals, and I'm getting my strength back."

"But – what about your arm? And the shoulder?"

His face clouds a little.

"That's going to take longer. The bullet smashed my collarbone and the shoulder blade. The surgeon sewed it all up, but the muscles don't connect to bone properly now."

I'm glad to have something to understand. I try to sound encouraging.

"It's early days. They might still mend."

"I doubt it," he says, then cheers a little. "But the nerves are starting to work again. My hand seemed completely dead at first, but the fingers are starting to move. Look."

We stand still. Concentrating hard, he manages to bring the first two fingers of his left hand hesitantly towards his thumb, then away again. It is such a tiny achievement that I want to weep.

"I know it's not much," he says. "But I'm working hard at it. They're getting quicker."

"That's wonderful."

I really mean it, because this tender beginning is like a green, slender shoot coming from a winter-blasted plant. Such tiny things will shape the way he can live. They are all he has, a frail armour to ward off despair. I so much want to help him. But I may not be allowed to. Worse, he may not want me to.

We walk on. Further up in the forest, we come to a fallen tree covered with moss. He moves towards it with some relief, and sits down.

"I usually rest here for a bit," he says in apology.

I sit beside him. A narrow stream runs close by. Yellow leaves are drifting down from the beech trees. A wren flits about in the branches of an almost bare hazel bush, watching us.

Perhaps he is waiting for me to say something, but I can find no words. Dread has come over me, and my hands are tightly gripped in my lap.

He takes a breath then says, "We have to face this. Your father was right, Hannah. You must not waste your time with me."

It is what I was dreading. He has accepted my father's words. He is casting me off. Anger rises in a hot tide, sweeping dismay aside. Is our future so easily dismissed, without even talking about it? Papa controls us, even here in this quiet forest. I cannot bear it.

"My time is my own," I burst out. "It does not belong to my father or anyone else. It is mine to waste as I choose."

He stares at me, astonished, then laughs.

"What a girl you are!"

But his face clouds again.

"Brave words are not enough, Hannah. Living means working. Earning money, growing food, building a house, riding, driving. I can do none of these things. I am no good to you."

I am still buoyed up with reckless fury.

"You can do other things. You never wanted to thatch roofs, anyway – you told me so. You said you wanted to be a musician and build harpsichords."

"You need two good hands to build a harpsichord."

"But your fingers have started to move. They will go on improving."

"With luck, yes. I don't know if they will ever be any use, though. I can't be certain."

I want to shake him, but that would not be fair. I am angry with fate, not with him.

He meets my eyes, but his gaze is troubled.

"You need a man who can take care of you. Provide for you and the children you may have. I am not just parroting your father's words, believe me, it is for your sake. You must forget me. Find someone else, while you are still young."

I get up from the log we are sitting on and move to the stream's edge, staring down at the running water. He has never said he loves me. The truth may be that he does not. It could be that he understands my feelings and shrinks from hurting me. If that is so, his injury will be the perfect excuse to end whatever there was between us. He likes me – I know that – but it could have been a passing attraction. James often talks of some Kitty or Polly who has taken his fancy, but he does not love them. If one of them loves him, he will escape from that at once and look elsewhere for his fun. Matthew is not so ruthless as James – he might have been touched by the unguarded way I showed my feelings. He might even share them.

But there is something else. He is a Royalist soldier. He fought and nearly died in the defence of his king. We are on opposite sides. The more I think about it, the more I can see that even if he does love me, such a love can have no future. He has the perfect excuse to free himself from me now. I must be brave. I have to accept it.

The grey sky and the thinning beech leaves swim with tears.

He is beside me. His hand is on my sleeve.

"Hannah – dear Hannah, what is it? Don't cry."

He is turning me gently towards him. I'm struggling to get my voice under control, but it is difficult.

"If you never loved me," I manage to say, "then I was mistaken. And – and stupid. I am sorry."

"Hannah!"

He sounds horrified.

"You *can't* think that! Don't you see – it's exactly *because* I love you that I must not spoil your life. I am no good to any woman. If I ever marry – which is unlikely – it can only be to some thick-witted slattern whom no able-bodied man will look at. But you are beautiful and intelligent and kind. You deserve a better life than I can give you. A better man."

Protest bursts out of me.

"I do not *want* better! You are the best, Matthew, surely you know that? I will never want anyone else. If you love me so much that you think you must cut me free, then love me less – *please* – love me less. But let me be with you. Don't send me away."

The fingers of his good hand smooth the tears from under my eyes then stroke their way gently down the side of my face. He lifts my chin, and his lips meet mine.

It is a long kiss – of a kind I have never known. At the end of it, I give a shaky sigh and lean my forehead against him. His right arm is holding me close. I have dreamed of this for so long – to touch him, to feel the strength of his body. And although he is injured, he is strong. The powerful spirit of him seems to flow through the fingers that press firmly on my ribs.

"Beautiful Hannah," he says. "I can never love you less. You are my world."

We kiss again, then part a little and gaze at each other in wonder at what has so suddenly been revealed.

He says, "I do not deserve such good fortune. But you must think about it carefully, my beautiful girl. Your father is going to be so angry."

"I know."

I am already trying to plan how to tell Papa, but my mind is shying off like a frightened bird.

We start to walk back along the path through the quiet trees, hand-in-hand, my pace matching his. Whatever happens in the rest of my life, I will always remember this moment.

When we come back into the yard, Matthew's father is unhitching his horses from a big cart piled with reeds. He glances at us across their chestnut backs and I know he has seen me release Matthew's hand. He makes no comment, just smiles in welcome.

"Can you stay for some lunch, Hannah?"

I realize with a shock that it must be getting late. Mama will be wondering where I am.

"I must go home," I tell him. "But thank you."

I turn to leave, but he has something else to say.

"If I am not mistaken," he says, "I should thank you, my dear – on my son's behalf. But be careful. Do not do anything rash. We live in dangerous times."

He leads his horses into the stable.

I head for home.

I have not told anyone yet, not even Elizabeth. I want these few hours to treasure my secret and keep it safe. I did not mention it at the midday meal, being a little late and hurrying to get food onto the table, but I will break the news this evening, before anyone hears it through gossip. When Papa knows the truth, trouble will begin. In my own mind, it has already begun, for I keep imagining what he will say. He will again forbid me to see Matthew, of course. And I will again disobey him.

Mama will want to know when we are to be married, because for her, love and marriage are the same thing. She will find it odd that Matthew and I have not yet spoken of it – but he and I both know there can be no question of marrying yet. He needs a long time to recover from his injury. It is enough to know we belong to each other.

His father's warning rings in my mind. "Do not do anything rash." But every choice before me seems rash. Papa himself is like a bonfire that threatens to burst into flame at the slightest disturbance. But I will have to disturb him.

I cannot remain silent, because Matthew's father will tell his wife. I do not know her, but she will probably see no reason for secrecy. She will tell her friends that a girl truly loves her injured son, and then everyone will know. The news will reach Papa through one of his many friends and acquaintances, and if I have not told him, his fury will be far worse. I must make the confession this evening, before he hears it from anyone else. But for these few hours, I want to hold my secret joy like a new-laid egg, warm and perfect, strong-shelled in my hand.

I am too late. He knows.

He strides into the kitchen and in front of all of us – Mama, Elizabeth, James and the younger ones – he roars at me, "Hannah Pomfret, I am ashamed to call you my daughter."

Mama gasps in shock, and he turns on her.

"You are surprised, I see. So our daughter has kept the truth from you as well. I never thought I would find such sinful deception and treachery in my own house."

Leah is frightened and runs to Mama, wailing. Jeffrey comes to fling his arms round me, but Papa catches him and turns him back with a slap on his bottom, shouting, "I did not tell you to move! Go to your mother and stay there!"

Mama draws Jeffrey close beside the weeping Leah, hushing his noisy tears. Her eyes keep darting back to me, full of terror. Will and Michael are staring down at their hands as though they have found something interesting there, meeting nobody's eyes. Elizabeth is silent in her corner though she is gazing anxiously at me. James is frowning, waiting for Papa's next words, which come at once.

"John Wainwright, though a Royalist, at least has honesty – unlike my own daughter, it seems. We met on the road and he stopped to tell me that his son, Matthew, intends to marry my daughter."

Mama gasps and puts a hand to her mouth, but Papa ignores her.

"John thought it best for me to know, before the news reached me through hearsay. I thanked him for his courage and for his honesty. But I have come home shamed by my own family."

His angry gaze is on me now.

"Hannah Pomfret," he thunders again, "what have you to say?"

I can find only one scrap of fact in my defence.

"We have not spoken of marriage, Papa."

It makes things worse.

"Do not lie to me!" he roars. "If you have no intention to marry, then what? Do you mean to live with him as a common whore? Have you sunk so low?"

My head is down. I am shaking. I dare not look at him, let alone say anything else.

When he speaks again, his tone is still bitter.

"John Wainwright, of course, cannot believe his luck. No presentable young woman in her right mind would take on his useless, one-armed son, who will probably never do a day's work in his life. So yes, Hannah, he will welcome you, to take a helpless cripple off his hands and see to all his needs. He and his wife must be thanking whatever mistaken God they worship."

He stares at me.

"I am waiting. What have you to say?"

I must not cry. Confronting my father is the first thing I can do for Matthew. Perhaps the only thing. I gather all my courage and tell him the plain truth.

"We love each other, Papa."

"Huh!" He snorts with contempt. "That is easy to say. Love is a convenient excuse for selfishness and lack of good sense. Lack of self-control, too, and lack of care for others. It is a mask for stupidity and self-indulgence. If you have no plans to marry, then what will you do? Live with this man in furtive shamefulness? Is that your plan?"

"No, Papa."

He pounces on the admission.

"In that case, why did you not tell your mother and me at dinner time today where you had been? Were you too ashamed to admit it?"

"I wanted just an hour or two. To think about it. To…"

I swallow hard.

"To what?"

"To – cherish it."

He closes his eyes and shakes his head.

"The devil walks in this room," he says.

With great deliberation, he gets down on his knees and joins his hands. We all do likewise. Leah and Jeffrey are silent, too scared to go on crying.

"Let us pray," he says.

A STRUGGLE FOR LIBERTY

When he had calmed down after some days of prayer, Papa asked me to give him my word that I would not see Matthew again. Rather than lie to him, I said I could give no such promise. Since then, I have ceased to exist in his eyes, and I fear his exclusion of me includes Elizabeth and Mama, in case they may be tacitly supporting me. We seem now to be a lower level of life that has proved itself unworthy.

Elizabeth is my one support, though nobody knows this. My lame, shadowy sister is easy to ignore, yet, sitting in her corner, she is constantly thinking. The things she says so often surprise me.

We are in the garden at the moment, gathering dry runner beans left on the withered growth, to keep as next year's seed. And talking about men.

"Women cannot vote and our opinion counts for nothing," Elizabeth says. "But men need us and love us. So we have a kind of power over them, but I don't think they know this. They are happy to be enchanted by a pretty woman and say they love her – and I am sure they mean it sincerely. But if a woman does anything surprising – as you have – it upsets them."

How does she know this?

"Look how quick they are to accuse us of witchcraft," she goes on. "They know we have the power to enchant, but it frightens them, too. They feel it must not get out of hand. That is why Papa is so angry – he knows he cannot control you. So you must be careful, Hannah. He will be looking for some other way to get you back into obedience."

"What kind of way?"

"I don't know. But there will be something. You can't expect him to give up. He is the head of the family. He is used to having his own way. And most of the time, his way is good, because even though he is stern, he cares for us. But now you have given him something very hard to accept."

"I know. I wish it didn't have to be like that."

Secretly, I can't quite agree with her. Matthew has never thought I bewitched him, as far as I know. He was prepared to live without me because of the injury that has partly disabled him, so he could not have been under any spell.

I tell her, "I don't think all men are like that."

She drops a handful of beans into the basket and smiles.

"Of course you don't," she says. "But then, you are in love. I never will be, so I just watch and learn. And keep quiet, because the way I look, people may easily think I am a witch."

"I won't let them," I promise.

Whatever happens in my life, I will always love my wise sister and make sure nobody harms her.

Though Papa and James treat me as invisible now, I listen more carefully to their overheard conversations, which include Will and Michael, since they are growing older. All four are very much taken up with the question of what will happen to King Charles.

Slightly against my will, I find it horribly fascinating. Parliament does not know what to do. They urge the King to agree that they have a right to pass laws and rule the country, but he will not. Although he is their prisoner, he is still the royal head of state, and sees all common men as inferior. So he is a total blockage to Parliament's plans. It seems more and more likely that they will have to condemn him to death, though there is no law on the statute book that he can be said to have broken.

"They will find one," Elizabeth says. "You'll see."

Matthew and I are beside the stream in the forest that we think of now as our special place. He does not wear the sling any more, because he says he must make the injured muscles work. But I can see that trying to do that is painful.

Sitting on the mossy log, he reaches down to a dandelion growing beside his foot, one of the few plants still in bloom as winter draws nearer. He tries to pick its yellow flower with his left hand, and he struggles hard to bring his forefinger close enough to his thumb to close on the soft stem. I hold my breath for him, willing it to happen.

The finger and thumb come hesitantly together. He gives them an impatient push with the other hand, and when he tries again, the dandelion stem parts. He presents me with the golden blossom like a trophy, smiling in triumph.

"Magic!" I say. "Wonderful!"

I raise my face to his and our lips meet. I want this connection to last forever. I want to be one with him, I want to know all of his body, not just his face and his sleeves and his unseen feet inside their boots.

Our kissing goes on, then the breath goes out of him in a long sigh. He says, "Oh, Hannah. Magic is what we need."

My white linen cap has fallen off, and he strokes my untidy hair.

"That is what I was fighting for," he says. "The magical things. Music and poetry and the lovely works of God."

"Like dandelions," I say, looking at the ragged blossom he gave me.

"Dandelions," he agrees. "And kings."

For a moment, there is a twinge of tension, then he adds, "Yes, I know. King Charles made terrible mistakes. But – royal descent goes back through history like a golden thread. Kings and queens are different from us. Special and strange. Like giants or monsters or ancient gods."

Because I love him, I am swept away by his words. But what ancient gods does he mean? The Catholic Church is much older than our Puritan one, but Papa says it is full of superstition and greed. I don't know what to believe. I look at the pattern of bare twigs against the white clouds and wonder why they are so lovely, but I do not know what God made them. I cannot guess what power it was that created the rocks deep under our feet, and the tumbling stream and the ever-changing shape of the moon.

Lord, if it is sinful to wonder, forgive me.

I am already sinful. I sin in my mind with Matthew all the time, and love each second of doing so. I want to be so close to him that there is nothing between us. As close as dandelion petals are to the autumn air that touches them all over.

Papa comes into the garden. I have just finished hanging up washing, so I pick up the basket and turn to go back to the house, but he stops me.

"Hannah. Please do not go away."

I stay and face him because I must, but I remember Elizabeth's words and I am prickling with suspicion.

"Your mother and I are worried about you," he says, "as I think you will understand. You are fifteen now. Next year you will be sixteen. Your mother points out to me that girls of that age are young women and feel the bodily impulses that come with adult life. She says it is natural for you to look with favour on whatever young man should happen to come your way."

Ah, I see. Mama has been trying to defend me. But she has got it wrong. Matthew is not a chance happening. I start to say something, but Papa holds up his hand.

"I do not wish to hear arguments. I am prepared to accept that your irrational behaviour may have been caused by the workings of nature. At this stage of your life you may not fully understand the sensations you are feeling. So I am prepared to overlook your current folly as an act of inexperience."

He pauses, but I am frozen with caution and say nothing.

He goes on, with sudden kindness, "You are still my daughter, a well-meaning girl and, I think I may say without the sin of pride, beautiful."

He pauses again. I have to say something.

"Thank you, Papa."

He frowns. "I hope you understand what I am saying to you."

"Yes, Papa."

But I do not know what this is leading to.

"I would like to see you in a good, stable marriage, Hannah. I am prepared to overlook your past indiscretions and help you to achieve this."

He puts his hand on my sleeve, which is very unusual, and makes an appeal.

"Do not regard me as an ogre, Hannah. I want the best for you."

Suddenly I ache with pity for him. It is not his fault that he cannot understand my love for Matthew. He is trying his best to be kind.

I say, "I know you do, Papa. Thank you." On a daring impulse, I add, "I do love you."

He nods a couple of times, and says, "I am glad to hear it. I hope it will lead to an improvement in the present unhappy situation."

He turns and goes back to his workshop.

That was three days ago. I am sweeping the boys' bedroom floor. My mother comes running up the stairs, excited. "Hannah," she says, "put on a clean dress and a fresh apron, quickly. We have a visitor."

"Who is it, Mama?"

"A friend of your father's. He met him in the town and brought him home. It's lucky we made a cake this morning. They are downstairs in the front room."

This is very unusual. Papa regards social visits as an expensive waste of time, and we only use the front room for prayers and special occasions. But of course, this may be a wealthy client or some elder of the church with serious matters to discuss. I put on my newest dress and a clean apron, and pin my hair back under a fresh white cap.

But it is neither a client nor a church elder. Sitting on one of our straight-backed chairs is thick-set youngish man with a broad, pink face, clasping a sack on his knees. It looks as if it contains something solid and heavy. He gets to his feet as we come in and shakes hands with my mother, then hands her the sack.

"I brought you a leg of pork, Mrs Pomfret. A small contribution to the household."

"Goodness," says Mama, holding the sack in both hands. It is slightly smeared with blood. "A whole leg? How very kind."

A leg of pork is more meat than we normally eat in weeks. We usually use cheap cuts like brisket or neck of lamb, with lots of vegetables.

"Not at all, not at all," the man says, smiling. His upper front teeth are missing.

He sees that I have noticed and indicates the gap with a cheerful wave of his hand.

"Small accident with a poleaxe butt," he says. "Otherwise sound in wind and limb."

Papa introduces him.

"Hannah, this is Samuel Grigson. A butcher by trade, as you will gather. And, I may say, a very successful one."

I know now what he meant in the garden when he spoke of an improvement in the situation. He thinks I will accept this butcher instead of Matthew. It is so grotesque that I almost laugh.

Samuel Grigson is looking me up and down as though appraising a prime heifer. He has traded a leg of pork for the chance of courting me, and wants to make sure he has a good bargain.

Papa turns to him and says, "Samuel, this is my daughter, Hannah."

I curtsey, but the man takes my hand in a powerful grip and shakes it heartily.

"Delighted to meet you, Hannah."

I want to wipe my hand on my apron, but know I mustn't. I turn to follow Mama into the kitchen. But that is not the plan, of course.

"Don't go, Hannah," says Papa. "Sit down."

He indicates the chair that faces Samuel Grigson. Reluctantly, I obey.

"So how is the butchery trade, Samuel?" Papa goes on, inviting him to set out his wares.

"Can't complain," he says. "I killed four good pigs this morning, and ten chickens. I've an excellent reputation, though I say it myself. Do you like chicken, Hannah?"

"Sometimes."

I do not want to speak to him.

"And you help your mother run the house?"

"Yes."

Mama comes in with a laden tray and sets it on the table. I get up to help her, but Papa again prevents it.

"Never mind about that. Sit down. Tell Samuel a little about yourself."

"There is nothing to tell."

"Now, come along," Papa says. "You are a capable girl."

He turns to the butcher. "She can read and write, you know," he says with pride. "Taught herself when she was quite young."

"Very commendable," Samuel says. "Though I don't look for book-learning in a woman."

I doubt if he has any himself.

Mama is handing plates round. "Cherry cake," she says. "Made this morning. Would you like beer or apple-drink? We had a good crop of apples this year."

"I'll take beer," Samuel says, then turns back to me. "Are you a cook, Hannah?"

"I help Mama."

"She's an excellent cook," says Mama. "She has a good hand for pastry, and she makes lovely soups and stews."

"Splendid," says Samuel.

I shake my head at the offered slice of cake and sip a glass of apple-drink, wondering how I can escape. I suppose Mama saw this as a way to heal the rift between Papa and me. She was terribly wrong. And now I am locked in this awful comedy.

Papa and the butcher are discussing skins and leather, but all the time, Samuel Grigson's eyes are running speculatively over my face and my body. They dwell on the front of my white apron as though he is imagining my secret breasts under my dress, and my face flames with embarrassment and fury. There is only one man who will see my body and run his hands and his lips over every inch of my skin when the clothes fall to the floor unnoticed – and he is not this butcher.

The conversation about leather comes to an end, and there is silence. Samuel glances at me again, then asks Papa, "Is she always quiet like this?"

Quiet, I think. Aha. This is the perfect excuse. Yes, that's it. I am not very well. I am never very well. I am an ailing specimen, a totally unsuitable wife for a vigorous butcher. Papa has started to say what a fluent speaker I am, but I stand up with a hand to my head, looking faint.

"You must forgive me," I murmur. "I have a terrible headache."

Samuel Grigson frowns and asks, "Do you get headaches often?"

The lie comes easily.

"Yes, very often. Almost every day. If you will excuse me, I really must go and lie down."

Papa glares at me in fury as I leave the room. Mama is staring down at her lap, nervously fingering her bonnet strings.

All of them will hear the back door open and my flying

footsteps going across the yard, but I don't care. I run through the garden to the top gate and then out to the field, where a sun as red as pork blood is hanging above the woods. Run and run.

RESOLUTION

I have stayed out for a long time. The sun has gone and the colour in the sky has faded. It is almost dark. I come quietly back across the yard and hope nobody will hear me lift the latch of the kitchen door. But I cannot get to the bedroom I share with Elizabeth without going through the living room, because the narrow, curling stairs go up from behind a door in the corner. And my parents are waiting for me in tense silence. So is James.

Papa wastes no time.

"Who do you think you are? Do you imagine you can live like some princess, expecting money to come from trees – or from me and your hard-working brother? Your rudeness this afternoon was disgraceful. By what right do you imagine you may pick a husband of your own choice, with no regard to whether he can provide for you?"

Anything I say will only make things worse. I stare at the floor and wait for these awful minutes to pass.

Mama sighs. "Oh, Hannah," she says. "Why are you are so obstinate?"

I can't reply.

"Go upstairs and stay there," Papa orders. "I am excluding you from our prayers until you apologize. You do not deserve to be a member of my family. And God will not want your false devotions."

I stumble upstairs in the dark without a candle. The door of Will and Michael's room closes quietly, and I know they have been listening.

Papa has stripped me of connection to God. I am more alone than I ever have been in my life. The long hours of self-control give way to tears and I grope blindly across the floor to the bed and to Elizabeth. She puts her arms round me.

"You are not alone," she whispers. "He cannot debar you from God."

I can't speak. But she, like the boys, has been listening, and she understands.

"We do not have priests who claim to represent God on earth," she reminds me in a quiet murmur. "We believe everyone is in touch with Him. That is what our religion is about. Papa knows this."

She is right. Slowly, my heaving sobs begin to subside.

"Put your nightgown on and come to bed," my sister says. "It will seem better in the morning."

How strange it is that she is younger than I am. She seems so much older and wiser.

We sit round the dinner table, waiting for Papa to come in and say Grace. My hands are gripped together in my lap and my head is bowed. My father comes through the door, but I dare not look at him. I stayed away from prayers this morning, as I was told, and have not seen him since last night.

He sits down then says, "Hannah, you may rejoin us at prayers from this evening onward. In my anger – which was and remains fully justified – I was hasty. But I cannot debar you from communication with God, who alone may bring you to see sense."

"Thank you, Papa."

I am careful not to look at Elizabeth, though I saw her limp into the workshop this morning. She was there for at least five minutes.

Papa closes his eyes and begins to say Grace.

That was three days ago. Since then, Papa has spoken no further word. I go about the usual household tasks mindlessly, like a dog running in a treadmill to turn a spit. All the while, my mind is away in the forest with Matthew.

This morning, a clear thought comes.

I have nothing to lose.

My hands pause in their wringing of wet clothes over a bucket in the yard, then continue with new energy. I know what I must do.

This time, I go to the front door and let the heavy knocker drop with a single bang.

A woman answers it. Her hair is dark but streaked with grey, and she wears a rose-coloured shawl round her shoulders, fastened with a brooch. She looks questioning for a moment then realizes who I am and smiles.

"Goodness!" she says. "How very nice to see you. Come in, my dear. I am Matthew's mother."

I follow her across the dim hall where coloured light falls across the stone floor from a stained-glass window above the door. She is leading the way to the kitchen.

"John!" she calls. "Matthew! Hannah is here!"

Mr Wainwright comes out of the study room and shakes my hand.

"Hannah," he says, "I am so glad you came."

Matthew is making his lopsided way down the stairs as fast as he can, looking anxious.

"Has something happened?"

"Not really," I tell him. "It's just that…"

"Come and sit down, both of you," his mother says. "It is warmer in the kitchen."

A lidded pot steams quietly on the stove, and yes, it is warm. We sit round the scrubbed table.

Mr Wainwright says, "I am sorry if breaking the news to your father caused trouble, Hannah. But we met face-to-face in the town, and I thought it best to tell him, rather than let him hear the news through gossip and wonder why I had held my tongue. But it came as a shock to him."

"I'm glad you did, though."

And it is true. Telling him myself would have been worse.

Matthew asks, "Is he getting used to it?"

"Not really."

I tell them about Samuel Grigson. It seems almost funny now, and Matthew's parents laugh. But Matthew looks unhappy.

"Samuel can offer you everything you need," he says.

"And nothing I want," I retort.

"Brave words!" his father says.

But words are easy and courage is not enough.

Matthew's mother is more practical. She says, "My dears, I am delighted for you both. But Matthew cannot look after you, Hannah. At least, not yet."

"But I am getting better," Matthew says quickly, "I was at the harpsichord this morning, and I can strike single notes with my left hand. I'll learn to play again, I know I will. And I can teach music. When I get strong enough, I can build and repair harpsichords. I've been thinking of how to make clamps to grip the work until my hand is stronger."

"Teaching is a possibility," his father says thoughtfully. "Rich people like their daughters to play an instrument. They think it's an accomplishment. Even as you are now, we might find you some pupils."

"Yes, but that is in the future," Matthew's mother says. "And the difficulties are here and now."

She turns to me.

"My dear, I don't wish to pry, but does your father know that you and Matthew mean to marry?"

I shake my head, blushing.

Matthew admits, "We haven't actually talked about marrying."

"That's all very well," his father says. "I know you feel things are very uncertain, and I don't blame you for that, but you are putting Hannah in a difficult position. Her father is a respectable man. He will not want it said that his daughter is living as a concubine."

Matthew half-rises from his chair, outraged. "There is no question of—"

"I am not insulting you," his father says. "I have no doubt of your decent intentions. But we must face the facts. People will talk. And Hannah's own home is, I suspect, becoming difficult for her because of her love for you. Is that right, Hannah?"

I nod, embarrassed.

Mr Wainwright goes on, "The pair of you seem untroubled by the difference in your religious backgrounds, which I am glad to see – but our support for the King is unacceptable to Hannah's father. It puts Hannah in a very awkward position."

"I know," Matthew says. "I think about it all the time."

His father looks at him carefully. Then he turns to me.

"Hannah, tell me something. Be honest. If some good fairy could give you the life you really dream of, what would it be? A nice house? Land, stables, servants? Pretty clothes? These are what most girls long for."

He is right. I used to dream of such things – but that is all it was, an idle dream. I know that now. The truth is simpler.

"I want to be with Matthew. That's all."

Matthew puts his undamaged hand over mine and says, "We belong together."

"Isn't that lovely!" Mrs Wainwright says, head on one side in a happy smile.

Her husband gives her a slightly disparaging look.

"Lovely indeed," he says. "But there are practicalities."

She waves her hand as if flicking them away.

"Oh, I know that, but it's quite easy. The girls have married and gone, so we've space upstairs. Matthew and Hannah can live here – at least until Matthew is better. Can't they?" She doesn't wait for a reply, but turns to me. "You'd be near your home, Hannah, so you could go on helping your mother if she needs it."

And I'd still see Elizabeth. It sounds wonderful.

"You are so kind. But Papa—"

Matthew's father has had enough of Papa. He glances at the grandfather clock and pushes his chair back from the table.

"There is a lot to discuss," he says. "But I have work to do. You are welcome to stay, Hannah – I'm not chasing you away. But I must get on."

He goes out. Matthew, too, stands up.

"Let's go for a walk," he says.

On the way up to our place in the forest, he hardly speaks, and I don't know what he is thinking. Perhaps he does not want to live in his parents' house and depend on their support. But what else can we do? It will be a long time before we can think of finding a place of our own. In my heart of hearts, I am not sure it will ever happen. It may be that Matthew is not sure, either.

Winter is coming. The trees are bare now, and the sun is pale and cold. At the mossy log by the stream, a robin hops about, perhaps hoping we have something for it. I must remember to bring some breadcrumbs next time.

Will there be a next time? Suddenly I am swept by doubt all over again. Matthew turns to face me as though he has something to say. Perhaps this is the end. His father's words may have persuaded him that it is all too difficult, and he is going to say goodbye. But strangely, he stoops to lean his good hand on the log for support and starts to lower himself onto one knee. I am alarmed. Is he in pain? But when he looks up at me, his face is charged with determination. When his balance is secure, he takes a deep breath.

"My very dear Hannah," he says. "Damaged as I am, and unable to offer you any certain future, I have no right to ask you this. But – will you do me the great honour of becoming my wife?"

"Oh!"

The breath goes out of me in shock and joy.

"Yes, I will. Of course I will. I love you so much."

He breaks into an incredulous smile and clambers to his feet, then takes me in his arms.

"I did not dare to ask," he says after our long kiss. "I was so afraid you would say no. It would have been the end of everything, so I delayed. But now…"

He spreads his hands, and I finish the sentence for him.

"It's all beginning."

THE KING

Matthew has come with me to break the news to Papa.

I'd half hoped that the workshop would be empty – he might have gone into town on business. But we can see him through the small window, his head bent over what he is doing. Perhaps it is as well. I am sick with dread, but delay will not make it any easier.

He looks up as we open the door, and his eyes narrow. He lays his knife and a piece of leather down on the bench but says nothing. My heart is pounding.

"Papa—" I begin. But he holds up a hand to silence me, looking at Matthew.

"Speak for yourself, young man."

Matthew takes a step forward, standing as straight and proud as his damaged shoulder allows. When he speaks, his voice is steady.

"Sir, I have come to tell you that I have asked your daughter, Hannah, to marry me. And she has accepted. I humbly ask if you will give us your blessing."

I hold my breath at such a daring request. Papa does not reply, but his eyes are fixed on Matthew's. A wordless struggle is going on, not so much between the two of them as in my father's own mind. Matthew returns his gaze steadily.

"You have courage," Papa says. "Or else you are a fool."

Matthew makes no answer.

I know from long experience that Papa's anger simmers slowly, but boils over fast. His voice is tight when he goes on.

"You ask my blessing. Have you any idea what that means?"

The speed and force of his words increases.

"You come here, cocksure, assuming that I will ask the approval of God the Father for a union that will take my daughter out of the true church and give her to an incompetent cripple who does not share our faith. Can you for one moment imagine that I will grant this request?"

Matthew somehow remains calm.

"I cannot expect your approval of me or of my family, sir. I know that, and I do not ask for it. I only hoped that you would see fit to invoke God's blessing on my union with Hannah, whom I love dearly. I am sorry if I have offended you. Hannah, I will see you tomorrow."

He turns to leave.

"Wait," Papa says. He is frowning.

"No man has the right to exclude another from the love of God – I accept that. The Papist priests are the only humans arrogant enough to believe they represent God on earth."

"My family are not Catholics," Matthew says.

"I am aware of that. Kneel down, both of you."

We kneel on the stone floor before Papa, who joins his palms and bows his head.

"May the blessing of Lord God Almighty be upon these erring children who have taken it upon themselves to follow the path of lustfulness. Through your infinite mercy, may they be healed and forgiven."

We do not move.

"In our ignorance and unworthiness, may all men be brought to the everlasting light of God. Bless, I pray, my daughter Hannah and her chosen," he pauses fractionally, "husband. Through the grace of our Lord Jesus Christ. Amen."

"Amen," we whisper.

By the time Matthew has managed to get to his feet, Papa is back at his bench, pulling the piece of leather towards him and picking up his knife. We both thank him, but he makes no answer and does not look up as we leave.

We go across the yard to the kitchen.

Mama puts her hand to her mouth at the sight of Matthew, but I tell her quickly about Papa's blessing, and she says, "Oh, thank the Lord. I am so glad."

"I am glad, too," Matthew says.

Elizabeth comes from her corner and kisses us both.

"Hannah, how wonderful!" she says.

The words she probably spoke to Papa after he excluded me from family prayers have done me a greater service than she realized.

Jeffrey and little Leah come up to kiss me and chatter, not understanding what has happened but happy that something nice is going on. It seems for a moment as if everything is untroubled and happy, although the future is so uncertain.

"Have you two had anything to eat?" Mama asks. "We've long finished dinner."

When I shake my head, she starts cutting slices from the loaf that is still on the table, together with butter and cheese and two late apples that are still good.

"Sit down, sit down," she says.

She keeps smiling at Matthew in a shy, astonished way, as if he is some kind of miracle. Which, of course, he is.

I offer a silent prayer of thanks.

Matthew has gone home and I am washing the dishes. Mama is full of the questions she did not ask when he was here. When will the wedding be? What does he intend to do for a living? Where are we going to make our home? I don't know any of the answers.

Will and Michael come in from school and the little ones run to tell them the news.

"Hannah is going to be married!" Jeffrey shouts, and Leah says, "Mattoo came, Mattoo came!"

Will looks alarmed and asks, "Does Papa know?"

He and Michael are astonished to hear about the blessing. I can still hardly believe it myself.

James comes in from Papa's workshop, grinning.

"Well, Hannah," he says. "Your intended husband has the cheek of the Devil, it seems. Are you really going to get married?"

"Yes. We really are."

He shrugs. "Good luck to you, then. You'll need it."

But he has more important news to tell.

"Have you heard? The army has moved the King to Hurst Castle. They are demanding that he be put on trial."

He smacks one fist into the other and laughs.

"Now we shall see! This is the beginning of the end for the Royalists!"

Michael asks, "Where is Hurst Castle?"

"Near Carisbrooke on the Isle of Wight, where he was before. And Hurst is almost an island, because a river washes all round it. There's no way in except the entry gate, so he can't escape."

Elizabeth asks, "What crime will the King be accused of?"

"Treachery," says James. "He conspired with the Scots, encouraging them to invade England. He has betrayed his own country."

"But his father was the ruler of Scotland as well as England," Elizabeth objects. "And does he not have the Divine Right of Kings, to do exactly as he likes?"

James looks a little less happy. "That is the whole trouble," he admits. "He will go on wearing that right like a suit of armour unless we can show it to be illegal. At the moment, there is no crime on the statute book that he can be accused of. But we have good lawyers working on it."

Michael asks, "If he is proved guilty, will he be imprisoned for life?"

"No," says James. "While the King lives, he is the ruler of England, no matter what he is guilty of. Parliament cannot govern the country unless Charles signs an agreement that he will share his power with them. But he will never do that. We wish he would, because then there would be a way forward. As it is, we are stuck with a hopeless problem."

"So what will happen?" Michael asks.

"If the King goes on being so obstinate," James says, "there is only one thing we can do. We will cut his head off."

I feel momentarily sickened, but it is best not to say anything. I go out into the cold garden, where the winter sun hangs low behind the trees, but it brings no comfort. Even the cawing rooks sound triumphant.

Another Christmas is over. Public festivities are still forbidden, so it has been a dull affair – but Matthew's house was defiantly garlanded with holly and yew, and full of people. His sisters and their husbands came, with a toddler and a baby. The sisters looked at me with some reserve at first, but they became friendly. They will be staying until after the New Year. I am not excluded, but it has been difficult to see much of Matthew.

King Charles has been moved to Windsor Castle, near London. They raised the drawbridge and closed the heavy, iron-studded doors, so nobody from outside can get in. James says Charles brought it on himself through being so obstinate.

Matthew and his parents are, of course, deeply distressed by what is happening, but they tactfully refrained from mentioning it when I visited them. My help wasn't needed in the kitchen but I played games with the children and kept them occupied. It snowed, which delighted them, but when we came in Mr Wainwright was sitting by the fire, and his face was full of anxiety until he looked up and smiled.

Compared with such great events as the execution of a king, our coming wedding early in February is a trivial thing, but it is keeping us busy. Elizabeth, Mama and I are in a frenzy of stitching, because they say a bride must have proper linens and clothing to bring to her new home. It has taken me by surprise, and I wish we did not need to make these frantic preparations. Perhaps I have something of Papa's respect for simplicity, for I feel embarrassed by such a fuss over things that are not essential.

Although I am longing to be with Matthew as his wife, I secretly wish we did not have to celebrate our union in public. It raises so many difficult questions. Somebody has to "give me away" – though it makes me sound like a sheep or a parcel. It should be Papa who does this, but he has not said yet whether he will come to the wedding, and I dare not ask him. If he does not, I don't know who can stand in for him. James would doubtless refuse, and I would never ask him. Mama has a brother, Uncle Edward, but he lives in a place called Suffolk and I barely remember him from a single visit when I was quite young.

The greater affairs go on. The King is to be put on trial very soon. He will conduct his own defence, Matthew told me, so he is drawing up a detailed legal argument, stating his right to rule. That also means his right to stay alive, because for him, to live and to rule are the same thing. James says King Charles cannot possibly win the case. Papa probably agrees, for he said at prayers this morning that we must be charitable in victory.

Heavy snow fell again last night. Matthew and I have ploughed our way almost knee-deep through its heavy whiteness on the way to our forest place. This time, I have brought stale bread and a pocketful of corn for the birds, and they are pecking about quite close to our feet. The death of a bird from hunger is a tiny thing compared with the death of a king, but perhaps my simple world is closer to sparrows and wrens than it is to powerful men.

Matthew and I are standing together with our arms round each other. My face is buried in the warmth of his neck, breathing the lovely smell of him. But he knows I am troubled.

"What is it, my love?" he asks. "Tell me."

It is hard to explain, but I have to try. I look up at him.

"I hate what is happening, Matthew. About the King, I mean. It seems so dreadful – yet I cannot blame my father for his beliefs. I am on neither one side nor the other. It seems so …" I grope for a word, "so *feeble*. It makes me ashamed."

"Thousands of people feel as you do," Matthew says. "When I was a soldier on the march, people in some places cheered us and in others they shook their fists. But more often the roadside was empty. People were attending to their own business, and if they thought about the war at all, they just hoped it would soon be over."

"I'm not trying to shut my eyes to these things, Matthew. I just wish I knew where I stand."

He kisses me again.

"Don't worry about it. You are your own sweet self, just as the wild birds are their own selves. They are the way God made them. There is no shame in that."

I can't accept what he says.

"I am a human being, Matthew, not a bird. I have a brain, just as you have. I just want to work out what to think."

"Yes, of course. I didn't mean…"

I'm going on.

"Birds know nothing of any king or what is in store for him. But I *do* know. I cannot un-know, even if I wanted to."

He sighs.

"Perhaps you are right. I sometimes wish I'd never got involved, even though I'm still sure we need a royal head of state. And yet – going into battle for what you are sure is good is a kind of duty. You can't stand aside and let it happen without you. War is weirdly exciting."

I am not persuaded. Perhaps women are different. If we did not get on with growing food and rearing children and keeping everything going, there would be nothing for soldiers to come back to. All their fighting would be pointless.

Snow has started to fall again. White flakes are wandering through the bare tree branches, settling on our dark coats and covering the small footprints of the birds.

Matthew turns to me and slips his hand inside my coat. A thrill runs through me. His mouth covers mine and with closed eyes I feel the snow on my face and the close, warm pressure of his body that matches my own so exactly.

"I want you so much," he whispers. "But we have to wait."

"Yes."

But if he asked me, I would lie down in the snow and let him take off my garments down to my bare skin, and cover me with his injured, beautiful body.

Papa closes his Bible at the end of evening prayers and looks at us. He has an announcement to make.

"In three days from now," he says, "on the thirtieth of January, a just sentence is to be carried out on Charles Stuart, erstwhile king of this land. He has been condemned to death for his treachery in inviting the Scottish forces to attack England. We are about to see a change in the whole course of England's history. For the first time, it will be ruled by a Parliament that represents the people. Having helped in my small way to bring about this Parliament, I shall be present at the execution. And so will my family."

His eyes are on mine. The message is clear. I have consorted with a Royalist soldier, and this is my punishment. I must witness the death of a king.

Mama says nervously, "William, I really don't think I can—"

He holds up a hand.

"I do not suggest that you or Elizabeth will come. Leah and Jeffrey are too young for a journey to London, so they will stay here, in your care. Hannah and my three older sons will accompany me."

James is smiling in satisfaction and Will and Michael look excited, though they know better than to speak out of turn.

Papa turns to me and hammers home the lesson.

"You, Hannah, are choosing to leave my house in due course. This may be my last chance to show you what the misconduct of an arrogant and incompetent king can lead to."

Argument is useless. I bow my head and say nothing.

AN END AND A BEGINNING

We started out before dawn yesterday. A thaw has set in, so the horses made good progress, but it is bitterly cold. Last night we put up at a house in a place called Dartford, where Papa has friends, and were on the road again early this morning.

We arrived at this inn an hour ago, in a place called Southwark. James and Papa are in the stables, feeding the horses and rubbing them down. Will and Michael and I are in a big basement room with a lot of other travellers who will sleep here overnight. There is a stove with a flue that goes through the wall, and people jostle round to put pots and kettles on its iron top. It is warm in here, and very smoky, and the smell of all these people and their dirty clothes is awful. I've unpacked the basket of bread and cold meat and plum cake that Mama gave us. The boys are ravenously hungry so I give them each a slice of bread to stave off the pangs until James and Papa join us.

Here comes James, looking important.

"Papa is having a drink with some people he has met.

He may be joining them for a meal, so we are not to wait for him."

We sit down at the space I have been guarding at one of the tables.

"There's a bridge over the river Thames just a couple of streets away," James goes on. "Whitehall is on the other side of the river, but it's not far. We can walk there."

Michael says, "Good to rest the horses before we start back."

James doesn't bother to nod. He goes on, "A man I was talking to says we'd never get the carriage through the crowds anyway – there will be thousands of people. The place will be packed wall-to-wall."

I feel as if I am dreaming, but alas, I am not.

Whitehall is much wider than I'd imagined. It's as broad and open as a field, but with imposing buildings on both sides. And I have never seen so many people. It is like market day in Canterbury multiplied many thousand times. The people are jammed together as close as sheep brought in for shearing. Some of the boys and young men have climbed up trees, to get a good view. Men on horseback lounge at the back of the crowd, comfortably able to see over the heads of the massed people. Every window in the grand buildings is packed with faces staring out from brightly lit warmth. They will be the privileged ones and their friends. How astonishing it must be to live in these immense houses, with uniformed servants to attend to their every need! Several times on our way here, we had to stand back for a painted and gilded coach, the driver in leather gloves shouting at the crowd to get out of the way, flicking his whip to sting anyone slow to obey. On the roofs above the warm, brilliant rooms, people who have managed to climb up are perched astride the ridges like outsized starlings.

In the centre of the huge crowd is the broad, high wooden platform that has been built outside the Banqueting Hall.

"That's the scaffold," Will says.

"We know that," says James.

Will looks crushed, so I tell him, "I didn't know."

On the right-hand side of the scaffold is the wooden block at which the King will kneel. It seems horribly low. The poor man will have to crouch rather than merely kneel. I shut my eyes for a moment and try to imagine being in the forest with Matthew. But Matthew is not in the forest. He is here somewhere, with his father. He said it was the least they could do, to pay their respects to the King. I have been looking for him constantly, but all I see are the faces of strangers.

Peddlers are moving through the crowd, selling hot chestnuts and ale – and oranges, too, though they are expensive. Papa asks if a news-sheet can be bought, but the man shakes his head.

"Not today," he says. "Been banned. Might cause public disorder."

The sky is full of threatened snow and it is bitterly cold. I tuck my hands in my shawl, glad of my woolly mittens. We have been waiting for a long time now, and people are getting restive. The dreadful event was supposed to happen at half past ten, but it must be gone midday by now. Papa tells us to stay where we are, and goes to make enquiries.

While he is away, rumours circulate. There has been a delay. There may be a reprieve. No, there won't be a reprieve. The King has been taken ill and cannot be moved. Yes, he can be moved, someone saw him at the Banqueting House window just now. Ah, the poor man, wouldn't be in his shoes. There is a legal problem. Something to do with the King's will.

Papa makes his way back through the crowd. He looks displeased.

"A legal problem," he confirms. "They should have realized it before, and dealt with it."

"What's the trouble?" James asks.

"It seems that unless something is done, the throne will pass straight to the King's son, who will then rule as Charles the Second."

James thumps his forehead with his hand and utters a swear word.

"Then all this has been for nothing!"

Papa does not rebuke him for swearing.

"Fortunately it was realized in time," he goes on. "A Bill is being rushed through the Commons at this moment, to outlaw royal inheritance."

Michael asks, "What is a Bill?"

"It is a proposed Act of Parliament," Papa tells him. "There have to be three readings of any Bill before it can be agreed as a new law."

"But – won't that take ages?" Will asks.

"Normally, it would. But today, because the situation is urgent, the three readings have been heard one after the other."

The boys nod gravely. I say nothing, as usual. This last-minute scramble is so ludicrous that it seems like a horrible joke.

We go on waiting. The soldiers, armed with pikes, who stand side-by-side all round the scaffold, remain motionless, though they have been there for more than three hours now.

There's a sudden excited buzz, but it quickly fades to a tense hush.

The King has come out onto the scaffold, escorted by several important-looking men. His hair and beard, though still long and curling, look neatly trimmed. He is wearing a white shirt that seems quite bulky, perhaps because it is a cold day, and he seems strangely calm. He unfolds a paper with no hurry, and begins to read it. Nobody except those close to the scaffold can hear the words, but even from where I am standing, his voice sounds calm and fluent. I wish I knew what he was saying.

At the end of the reading, he folds the paper again and hands it to one of the men with him, who takes it and bows deeply.

King Charles kneels at the block, and yes, it is terribly low. He has to crouch down, in the position of a frog or a toad. The executioner has been standing back until now, holding the long shaft of his axe motionless, blade to the floor beside his left foot. Now he steps forward and takes up his position beside the block. He is wearing a black mask that hides his face

The King stretches out his hands as if in an agreed signal.

I shut my eyes.

The sound of the axe-fall is a single whack like a woodsman cleaving a log. A long, low groan comes from the crowd. Nobody cheers. Even James is standing very still with his head down, as though struck by something he had not expected to feel. The man next to Papa who was grumbling about the delay has his hand over his face. Countless people are weeping. A woman has fainted, and people are bending over her.

I risk a look at the scaffold, and wish I hadn't.

The executioner is holding up the King's head by its hair.

People standing close to the scaffold are reaching between the still-motionless soldiers to dip handkerchiefs in the awful lake of blood that is dripping over the edge. That sickens me afresh. The blood of a king is no more than a souvenir to take home and keep for a while. In time, the stained white cloths will be thrown away and forgotten.

I find I am in tears.

Curled up beside Elizabeth in our shared bed, I am so cold from the two days of travelling that I cannot stop shivering.

Elizabeth holds me close. "It's all right," she murmurs. "It's over."

"Yes."

"We finished your wedding dress while you were away," she goes on, trying to cheer me up. "I stitched white daisies round the neck. It looks so pretty."

I kiss her in thanks. I cannot tell her the awful thing my mind brings, like an over-eager dog. James said they are going to stitch the King's head back on its body, so the relatives and mourners can view him in his coffin.

It is so good to be with Matthew again, even if with his parents in their warm kitchen. His mother is ladling chicken broth into bowls. His father is reading a printed paper.

He asks Matthew, "Have you seen this?"

"No. What is it?"

"The full text of the words the King spoke on the scaffold."

I am sitting beside Matthew so we read it together. One sentence jumps out at me.

A subject and a sovereign are clear different things.

So to the very end, King Charles held to the royal privilege that set him above common men. I can't agree. In this, I think Papa is right; all men are equal in the sight of God.

Matthew has been struck by a different passage. He reads it aloud.

"*Freedom consists in having of government, those laws by which their life and their goods may be most their own.*"

He lays the paper down and says, "How wise he was! He knew people want to be in charge of their own lives and their own businesses."

"How brave, too," Matthew's mother says. "Someone told me he was wearing two shirts, one on top of the other, so that he would not shiver in the cold and make people think he was afraid. Eat your soup while it's hot."

Mr Wainwright takes a spoonful of soup and says, "M'm. Good."

He adds, almost casually, "We will have a king again, of course. Within a couple of years, I'd say."

"Will we?" I'm startled.

"Oh, yes. The Scots will see to that. After all, Charles

was the son of James the Sixth of Scotland, so they felt he was their king. They are furious that the English Parliament executed him without even asking them."

"It will happen," Matthew agrees. "It's just a question of when."

Papa has gone to town, so Elizabeth and Mama have made me try on the wedding dress. They move round me with pins, and I feel like a queen.

Elizabeth stands back a little, looking at the dress through narrowed eyes.

She says, "The sleeves are a bit long."

Mama says firmly, "Sleeves that come over the hands are ladylike. And she won't be wearing it to do the washing-up."

The dress is beautiful. The long folds of the skirt come to my feet, almost covering my old shoes, and Elizabeth's embroidered daisies edging the neck are so delicate that they do not remind me of what was done to the King. They are innocent daisies.

The wedding is to be in the Cathedral, which is used as a church again. The captured weapons have gone, and horses are not stabled there now. I don't know if Papa will come, and I dare not ask him. He does not like the Cathedral, but when I tentatively suggested to Matthew's mother that we might marry in our plain little Puritan church, she said, "My dear, you want to remember your wedding as a *beautiful* day."

She and Matthew's father have been very careful to respect my family's religion, so I could not object to this single mild rebuke. I am only one half of this marriage, and Matthew holds his beliefs more strongly than I hold mine. I do not mind this – I only know that I love him. And his parents have been so kind. A few days ago, his mother showed me the room that is to be ours, and it is bigger than any room in our house. It has high ceilings that slope down on either side of a dormer window looking out over the fields, and there is a large wardrobe with four doors, a washstand and a chest of drawers. There is enough space for a round table and two chairs as well as the big, curtained bed.

Mama put in a last pin and stands back to look at the hemline.

"That seems all right," she says. "Hold your arms up and I'll slip it off over your head. Shut your eyes in case of pins."

Elizabeth says, "It's a pity about your shoes. But they won't show."

This seems like a dream. I am standing in the Cathedral, faced by rows of people sitting on the chairs. Papa is beside me, wearing his black Sunday suit. He has done something wonderful. Peter Burton the cobbler came to our house this morning and said, "Your order, sir."

"Ah, yes," Papa said, and indicated me. "For my daughter, if you please."

And Peter put into my hands a pair of new-made white satin slippers.

I ran to embrace Papa, weeping with delight, but he simply said, "I hope they fit," then went outside to harness the horse.

The Cathedral looks bare because of the daylight coming through its replaced plain glass windows. The carved pews have gone and there are no statues or pictures. Perhaps that is for the good, if it makes Papa feel more comfortable. There are far more people than I expected. Elizabeth is my maid of honour, standing as straight as she can, her crutch half-hidden in the folds of her blue dress. Mama and little Leah have new dresses as well, and we made new shirts for the boys.

We are looking down the aisle to where the great doors stand open to the winter sunshine. A group appears in the doorway and starts towards us, dark against the daylight at first. But candles are burning in the height of the Cathedral, and faces become distinct in their glow. Matthew is at their centre, walking as straight and tall as he can. His father is on his right, Roger Blackburn on his left; I don't know the other men, and did not expect to. It does not matter. There will be so many new things now.

They have come close. Matthew's eyes are steady and

grey and calm, as I will always remember them. The words of the service begin. They fly up like white doves, out of the Cathedral to the fields and the sky, careful and beautiful yet full of their own freedom. As is my love.

HISTORICAL NOTE

Hannah's story takes place between 1647 and 1649, in the middle of the Civil Wars that had been dividing families and causing countless deaths since 1640. These wars were caused by the conflict between King Charles the First and the Protestant English Parliament, which had astonishingly new ideas about a more democratic form of government. Its session known as the Long Parliament began in November 1640 and lasted for four years. Before that, the king had been able to call the Parliament together or dismiss it when he chose, but the Long Parliament protected itself by passing a law stating that it could only be dissolved through the agreement of all its members.

This was a revolutionary change – and so were the Long Parliament's policies. It proposed that an elected government should give common men representation in the running of the country. This new idea ran through Europe like quicksilver, and the dissent it provoked gave rise later to the French revolution, which wiped out its royalty and made France into the Republic it is today. It also laid down the democratic principles on which the United States of America is governed. England, however, did not unite against its monarchy. King Charles was determined to preserve the Divine Right of Kings that gave him total power to rule as he wished, so he opposed the Parliament's idea with all his strength, and gathered a lot of support. Throughout Britain, people fought in defence of their conflicting principles.

Presbyterian Scots and the English Puritans were determined to abolish the power of the king, together with all the pomp and ceremony that royalty enjoyed, but Catholics and moderate Protestants tended to uphold the monarchy. The split between these views was so wide that it led to nine years of warfare between Parliamentarians (Roundheads) and Royalists (Cavaliers). The first war ran from 1642 to 1646.

The King's French wife, Henrietta Maria, went to France in 1644, to sell jewellery to raise funds for her husband's campaign against the Parliament. But money was not enough. Cromwell's New Model Army was a well-trained body far superior to the amateur soldiers on the Royalist side, and Charles lost the crucial battle of that first war at Marston Moor on 2 July 1644. Henrietta Maria, fearing for her children and herself, returned to France with her son and a newborn baby daughter, and never saw her husband again.

King Charles finally lost the First Civil War in 1646, but he sensed, correctly, that Parliament was not happy to see Cromwell's New Model Army becoming the controlling power in the land. Presbyterian principles became more severe. The banning of Christmas in 1647 and onward was very unpopular. Hannah, in her story, sees that public opinion is starting to veer towards support for the Royalists, defeated and badly organized though they were. Meeting Matthew makes her understand, as many people do, that both sides have values to defend.

In 1648 the remaining Royalist forces joined with the Scots and the short-lived Second Civil War began. It seems a long time to Hannah, anxious as she is about Matthew, who has gone to fight, but it lasted for less than a year. The Cavaliers had little chance. The New Model Army was effective and ruthless, and on 28 August 1648, the starving Royalist garrison in Colchester surrendered to Lord Fairfax. Despite this final defeat and his imprisonment, King Charles still would not compromise on his "Divine Right" to govern as he wished, and the Parliament could see no solution except to order his execution. The King was beheaded in Whitehall on Tuesday, 30 January 1649.

Hannah and Matthew will live though troubled times after the end of their story, for the Third Civil War began almost at once, in 1649, and went on until the final Parliamentary victory at the Battle of Worcester on 3 September 1651. The Parliament of Scotland, which had been furious at the English Parliament's execution of Charles I without even consulting them, had at once proclaimed the King's exiled son, Charles II, as their king. England, conversely, became a Commonwealth that lasted until 1653. After that it was a Protectorate under the virtual dictatorship of Oliver Cromwell until his death in 1658.

Had Cromwell been as skilled in diplomacy as he was in war, England might have remained a republic to this day – but he was abrasive and unlikable, and did his own cause no good. When he died, there was something like a collective sigh of relief, and the executed king's son, young Charles, was invited to return from France and rule as Charles II. He entered London on 29 May 1660, his 30th birthday, and was greeted by cheering crowds.

All legal documents of the time and onward are dated as though Charles II had succeeded his father in 1649, with no break. Officially, the nine years when England was a republic never happened. Although the Roundheads had won all three stages of the Civil War, the British people chose to have a king again, so in history, the crack is papered over. Yet the Parliamentary victory was a permanent one, for there was never any return to the absolute power of the monarchy.

ALSO AVAILABLE

By My Side

A SECOND WORLD WAR LOVE STORY

SUE REID

READ AN EXTRACT FROM
BY MY SIDE

By My Side

A SECOND WORLD WAR LOVE STORY

AMSTERDAM, 1942

7 JANUARY 1942

I'm not sure this is the usual way to start a diary. Not that I've ever kept one before. Anneke does. Once I asked her what she wrote in it. "Things I can't tell anyone," she said, rather too promptly. I felt a bit hurt when she said that. But now I feel I understand. Sometimes there are things you can't tell anyone. Not even your best friend. Something that you know might turn into something big. And you just know when that happens. And it can happen in the most ordinary, unsurprising way, on a day that begins like any other – like today.

After school Maarten and I cycled home. I'd been quite flattered that he wanted to accompany me. He's the cleverest boy in the class – and he said he'd help me with my maths homework. Saskia – who sits on one side of me at school, Anneke sits on the other – says that's because he likes me, but she would. Saskia is boy-mad. I'm not – I like lots of things.

We hadn't gone far when we began to quarrel. Maarten's a bit of a know-it-all. But isn't it strange how things happen?

If we hadn't been quarrelling we'd not have taken the wrong turning and I'd never have met Jan.

I only realized that we'd missed the turning when we found ourselves at Mr Breitkopf's shop. Only we could hardly see it for all the people standing in front of it. Maarten said we should go, but I wanted to find out what was happening. I'm nosier I suppose. Besides, I like Mr Breitkopf. Then the tall man in front of us moved aside and I could see old Mr B, his face terrified, cowering in his doorway. Some boys were jumping up and down, taunting him. "Jood. Jood." That wasn't all. Men wearing the uniforms of the Dutch police were watching them, grinning, arms folded. They did nothing to stop the boys. It made me feel sick. Let me be plain. Most of my countryfolk are good, decent people, but some belong to the Dutch Nazi party. And the Occupation has made them bold.

"You've got to do something," I hissed to Maarten.

He looked at me as if I was mad.

"What can I do?" he said.

"Stop them! He might get hurt."

"I can't!"

"Someone's got to!" I'd raised my voice and one or two people turned round and stared at me.

"No, I can't," he said again.

I looked at him. His face had gone red.

And then I understood. I felt a bit sick. It was as if he'd said aloud: "Because he's a Jew."

"Then I will!"

He grabbed at my arm. "Don't be stupid. They'll kill you!"

I shook him off. "Now you're being stupid!" I said. "They're only boys." I'd forgotten about the police.

"Katrien!"

"Oh go away, you coward." I pushed him away, wishing I felt as brave as I'd sounded. I was scared – truly scared. What did I think I was doing? A hateful little voice was whispering in my head: *Maarten's right, you know. Go home. It's none of your business.*

I'd nearly reached the front of the group when I heard a voice shout "No!" and I looked up to see a boy throw himself in front of the old man. There was a vicious crump and I saw the boy reel backwards, his hand held to his face. Blood was seeping through his fingers. "That will teach you to help a Jew!" a harsh voice growled. His fist drew back to strike again. That was enough for me!

"Stop it!" I shouted. "Stop!" My voice sounded very thin to my ears, but the man put up his fist and swung round. You should have seen his face. A girl – standing up to the police. It seemed to rouse the people near me. One man hastily hauled the boy to his feet, and another helped Mr B away. I stared back as bravely as I could, a vision of my soon-to-be-bloodied face like a mirror in front of my eyes. But to my surprise I heard the policeman laugh, his friend said "come on", and they slunk away like bored dogs to find someone else to torment. I thanked whoever was watching out for me for my lucky escape.

Then I ran up to the boy. He was leaning against the shop, his hand over his mouth. "Are you all right?" I said.

"You should thank this girl, lad," said the man who'd helped him. "You'd have got worse if she hadn't stepped in. You're very brave," he added to me.

"I know," the boy said through his fingers.

"Not as brave as you," I said – all the compliments making me feel rather embarrassed. The boy gave me a lopsided smile. The eyes he turned on me were startlingly blue. Not many people have eyes that blue. And it was that I think that made me feel sure I'd seen him before somewhere. I just couldn't think where.

The boy took his hand from his face and spat out some blood. His mouth was swelling fast.

I turned my head away. Looking at that face was making me feel a bit sick. I fished in my pocket for my hanky.

"Here," I said, handing it to him, "take this. It's quite clean," I added.

"Thank you," the boy said, taking it from me and gingerly mopping his mouth. I saw him wince. It must have hurt.

"That mouth needs seeing to," I said.

"Are you a doctor?" the boy said, his voice muffled through the hanky. I felt he was trying to make a joke and I was impressed that he was able to.

"My father's a doctor," I said. "He'll look at it for you." I put my hand lightly on his arm to encourage him. All the people who'd been watching had wandered away now, but the streets were far from quiet and we were getting some pretty funny looks. I knew I had to get him away. He couldn't stay there – not with a face like that.

He shook his head. "I'll be all right."

"It's not far," I promised. "I only want to help," I added, when he still looked doubtful.

He nodded. "OK." He held out his hand, saw it was bloodied and hastily withdrew it. "I'm Jan," he said. And it was as if something clicked in my memory and I knew that I had seen him before. At my school. I didn't really know him – only in the way younger girls know of older boys. He wasn't one of the boys girls hung around. But when I told him my name I could see it meant nothing to him, so I didn't say anything about school.

We hadn't gone far when Jan stopped and put a hand on

my arm. "What's wrong?" I asked. I glanced at his face. It was deathly pale.

"Can't you see them?" he whispered.

"Who?"

"Soldiers!"

"What?"

"Over by the railings."

Then I saw them. And I saw that they'd seen us.

I knew it was bad. They'd ask for our identity cards. I was used to this. It's part of living under Nazi Occupation. It had never worried me before. I'd hand over my card, they'd look at it, then at me, and hand it back. But this time it would be different. This time there would be questions. "*How did you come by that face, hein? You were in a fight? There was trouble at a Jew's shop today. We are looking for a girl and a boy. His injuries match yours.*" They'd take him away. And maybe me, too. And there was nothing I could do about it. And it was then I had this extraordinary feeling. That my brief act of courage was going to turn my world upside down.

"Run?" I suggested, as if Jan was able to.

"Too late," he muttered.

I looked over to see that one of the soldiers had already detached himself from the group and was walking towards us. Jan pressed the hanky back over his face to try and hide his injured mouth. The hanky was all bloody, though. He might as well not have bothered.

"You have been in a fight?" the soldier said as he reached us.

Jan was silent. So was I.

The German was waiting. One of us had to say something. But what?

"Maybe he fights over you? Your boyfriend." The German grinned. It wasn't what I'd expected him to say and to my annoyance I felt myself blush. I couldn't tell what Jan thought – I didn't dare look at him.

"You are a very pretty girl," the soldier said.

I was disgusted. He was our enemy. Did he think I cared what he thought?

"Cigarette?" The soldier took a pack from his pocket and held one out to me.

I gave him a cold stare. "I don't smoke."

"No?"

"I'm a schoolgirl."

"Ah, I see." My reply had disconcerted him. He'd taken me for an older girl.

"Well, maybe then…" His eyes turned from me back to Jan. They narrowed.

I felt a moment's panic. It was coming, the German was

going to take him away, and I'd not be able to stop him. I looked around. There were plenty of people in the street, but if they saw the desperation in my face they ignored it. I couldn't blame them. Who would want to step in and put themselves in danger? Over by the railings the German soldiers were prowling, like a pack of dogs who'd smelt blood. Any minute now…

"Katrien?" I swung round to see our neighbour, Mrs Mcicr, staring at us. My relief at seeing a friendly face was so great I nearly burst into tears. If anyone could get us out of this mess she would. She didn't waste time asking for explanations but marched straight up to the soldier. "Officer," she said. "I must get these children home."

Children! I'm nearly sixteen!

But for once I'd enough sense to keep what I thought to myself.

"You know them?" the German said, putting the cigarettes away in his pocket.

"I do," she said, though I felt sure she had never seen Jan before. I found myself praying he wouldn't ask her for our names.

"I see that I have made a mistake." But I saw in his eyes that he knew. No mistake. But for some reason he was letting us go. I tried not to think it had anything to do with me.

He glanced at me again. For a moment his eyes held mine. Then he smiled. "Take him home. His face needs cleaning up." He nodded and sauntered back to his friends. The soldiers seemed to settle. I heard one of them laugh.

Mrs Meier put a firm hand on each of our shoulders to lead us away. "Hurry," she said. Not that we needed urging. The soldiers were still lingering by the railings.

"Thank you," Jan said. "I am very grateful. But I must go now."

"Don't try to talk," she said quietly.

She doesn't want to know. She is wise.

It was only a short walk to our house. While Mrs Meier rang the doorbell, I waited on the steps with Jan. My stomach was bouncing around inside me. What was Mother going to say when she saw him? How would I explain where I'd been? Jan was looking up at the house. Suddenly I saw how it might look to a stranger. The narrow imposing house, gazing out on to the frozen canal. A house where well-to-do people live. The leafless trees, their bare branches reaching up to embrace the sky. Children, well wrapped up, sliding down the canal. The people walking slowly by its side – I saw how prosperous they looked, even now. I saw then how thin Jan's coat and scarf were. He swallowed. Was he nervous, too? I touched his hand to reassure him. He glanced at me and I saw again how blue his eyes were. Blue eyes and dark hair. I like that. It's unusual.

"Katrien?" I looked up to see that the door of our house had opened. Mother was standing there, staring at me. "Where have you been? I've been so worried." And then she saw Jan.

I don't think I'll ever forget the expression on her face.

His face was swelling nicely and there was dried blood on one cheek.

"Why! Who is this? Whatever has happened?" she got out at last.

"I found these two on the street," said Mrs Meier swiftly, popping round from behind us. "And the young man needs help. Margrit, I'll see you tomorrow. Goodnight, children." With a quick bob of her head she was gone.

"Perhaps you will explain, Katrien," Mother said. I'd pulled Jan in behind me before she could object. "Who is this, and where is Maarten?" She glanced back as if she half expected to see him lurking behind us.

I sought for something to say. "Mother, this is Jan – a boy at my school." I saw Jan's start of surprise, and I hurried on before he could say anything. "He got hurt defending Mr Breitkopf from some Dutch Nazis!"

"Oh, no!" she exclaimed. "The poor old man! Is he all right?"

"Yes," I said. "He got away."

Mother turned back to Jan. "You are a brave boy! Sit down – please – and take off your coat and scarf. I'll give your face a bathe. My husband can take a proper look at it when he gets back."

"I don't want to be any trouble," Jan said. I could sense how uncomfortable he was. His eyes wandered around the hall, staring at it. At the fine clock, the polished hall table.

"It's no trouble." A smile wavered briefly on her face. "Katrien, come with me."

Leaving Jan standing there, I followed Mother into the kitchen. I watched while she ran warm water into a bowl. Her back to me she said, "Katrien, I don't understand. Who is this boy? You've never mentioned him before. And what is this about Dutch Nazis?"

I felt as if I was being cross-examined. I seized on the one question I could safely answer. "They were bullying Mr Breitkopf and Jan stepped in."

"And Jan – what do you know about him?"

"He goes to my school." Or he did. A slight suspicion was forming in my mind, but I kept it to myself. I wasn't even sure I was right.

"Don't be silly, Katrien. You know what I mean. Who is he? Who are his people?"

"I've told you all I know. Anyway, does it matter?"

"Don't speak to me like that, Katrien."

"Well, didn't I do the right thing bringing him home? You always say we should help when we can!"

"I hope so," she said quietly. "I hope so." She turned to me. "And Maarten? Where is he?"

I shrugged. "I don't know. Probably run home to hide. He's a coward, Mother. He didn't even try to help." I remembered the expression on Maarten's face. I didn't like thinking about it. He hadn't helped him because he was a Jew.

"He's not a coward. Katrien, what could he do?" She sighed. "Don't be too hard on him. He's a nice boy."

I don't think he is, Mother. Not as nice as you think.

"Now we must go back to Jan." I followed her back into the hallway where Jan was waiting. He had taken off his coat and scarf, but he looked as if he wished he was a million miles away. I saw Mother try to smile as she dabbed water on his face. She told him again that he was brave, but I felt that she wished he was miles away, too. I saw how relieved she was when the front door opened and Father came in. He examined Jan's face carefully. "Nothing is broken," he said. "You've been lucky, young man. So," he said when he'd finished, "how did you come by this injury? It's a nasty one."

I opened my mouth to speak, but Father shook his head at me. "Let the lad speak for himself, Katrien."

"I was trying to protect Mr Breitkopf," he said. He shrugged as if protecting Jewish people was something he did every day.

"You're a brave boy," Father said, putting a hand on Jan's shoulder. "It is shameful what is happening. Shameful."

They went on and on about how shameful it was. I wished they'd stop. Couldn't they tell how uncomfortable they were making him? "I'd better go," he said at last, shifting from foot to foot. "My parents will be wondering where I am."

They offered him tea, food, but Jan refused it all. Even cake! Fancy refusing cake!

I went with him to the door. I was hoping he'd say something like: I'll see you at school, Katrien. Or: maybe I can walk you home tomorrow. But he didn't. Maybe it was just that my parents were standing nearby, breathing over us like dragons. Not that they needed to. I knew he was a nice respectful boy. I can't explain how I knew. I just did. Like you do.

It was only after he'd gone that I saw it. His scarf, lying on the floor. He must have dropped it in his haste to leave.

I picked it up and ran outside. I looked up and down the street. But of course he'd gone.

I've folded it up and put it on the chair so I won't forget it in the morning. It's pretty moth-eaten, lots of little holes in it. Mother would say it's only fit for the bin. I'll take it to school tomorrow and give it to him then. Maybe he'll be so pleased he'll walk me home.

8 JANUARY

I'm writing in an old school exercise book. It's lucky I found it, or I wouldn't be able to keep a diary. Paper's in short supply, like so many other things in Holland now. I'm squashing as many words on to the page as I can, to make it last. My brother, Pieter, says my writing looks as if a spider had fallen into an inkpot and crawled across the page! He has a nerve. His is no better.

I've found a place to hide it – under the mattress. It's pretty lumpy, so no one will know it's there even if they accidentally sit down on it.

I've pulled the eiderdown up to my chin. It's freezing!

Heating is another thing that's rationed, and the house is always cold. Mother *says* she turns it up in the living room in the evening but even if you sit on the radiator it feels barely warm at all.

But at least I feel full for once. Mrs Meier came round for tea. She brought some of her home-made biscuits. Pieter wasn't home, so I ate his share as well as mine. Mrs Meier's biscuits are famous! She encouraged me to eat up. "You're a growing girl," she said. Mother said if I go on like that I'll grow outwards as well as upwards. Mrs Meier just laughed. She's really nice. She asked after Jan, too. I told her I hadn't seen him. I expect his mother's kept him home, she said, but I saw the glance that passed between Mother and her.

I had to go to school on foot this morning. I couldn't find my bike. It was only when I was halfway there that I remembered where I'd left it. Outside Mr Breitkopf's shop. I felt like kicking myself. Someone would almost certainly have stolen it, and how would I confess to Mother and Father? It had been their present to me on my fifteenth birthday. I asked Pieter if I could borrow his, but he was annoyed that I'd woken him, and grunted that he needed it to get to university, before turning over on his side and going back to sleep again. My brother is so lazy. He'd stay in bed all day if Mother let him.

Of course by then I was late so I had to run all the way. As I dashed through the school gates I saw Maarten over by the bike racks. I pretended I hadn't seen him but he saw me and waved me over. Then I saw what was propped up next to him. My bike! I was so relieved but he wouldn't let me thank him, just shoved the bike at me and stalked off. Not that I care. I don't want to be friends with him any more. He let me down. I think he feels the same – for when I got into the classroom I saw that he'd moved his books to sit as far from me as he could without falling out of the window. As we were putting our books away at the end of the lesson Saskia leant across to ask what was up between us. I didn't tell her, of course. You don't tell Saskia anything unless you want everyone to know. She cannot keep a secret.

I looked out for Jan at school but I didn't see him – not once. Several times I thought I had but each time the boy turned round I realized my mistake. After a time I had to stop. I was getting some pretty funny looks. Mrs Meier must be right. His mother will have kept him at home. I'll try again tomorrow.

9 JANUARY

Maarten actually spoke to me today. He asked how I was getting on with my maths homework. He smiled, but it wasn't a very nice smile. I didn't answer him. At lunch he disappeared somewhere with Saskia. He made sure I saw, too. As if I care!

Later Anneke came over to perch on my desk. She asked me what was wrong between us. I shrugged and said we'd fallen out. "Why?" she asked.

"We quarrelled, Anneke, that's all," I said doodling with my pen on my exercise book so she couldn't see my face. She must guess that I'm holding something back but I don't want to talk about it – not even to my best friend. I'm finding out just what a friend a diary can be. You can write what you like and it will never ask awkward questions!

I've still got Jan's scarf. I'm wondering what to do with it. It's too worn for me to wear, but I don't want to throw it away. I looked on the timetable this morning to find out what classes he's in so that I could wait for him afterwards, but there are lots of older boys called Jan. Then I thought of stationing myself at the gate at the end of school to see if I could catch him then, but Anneke and Saskia were with me.

Maybe his family are keeping him at home for a few days. I've just got to be patient.

12 JANUARY

After school today I cycled over to Mr Breitkopf's shop. I don't know what drew me back there. I suppose I was curious to see it again. It's not his shop now, of course. Jewish businesses have been taken away from their owners and given to new ones. I heard Father talk about it. It's one more way the Nazis have found to torment the Jews. They've become very good at that.

I propped my bike up against a railing and walked over to the shop. I wondered what he'd been doing there that day, poor old man.

In the old days before the War began and spoilt everything Mother often used to bring me here. It was a treasure trove of all sorts of curious and wonderful things. I loved exploring it.

When Mother was being served Mr B used to slip me sweets from out of a big glass jar he kept on one of the shelves at the back. It makes me feel sad to think about that. The shop was closed for the day and the door was locked so I went up to a window and peered in. It looked musty and untidy as if no one had been there for a long time. Whoever owns it now isn't looking after it.

I got back on my bike and cycled away. I've been thinking a lot about Mr B. I wonder how he's managing now. It can't be easy for him. I doubt the Nazis gave him a fair price for the shop. More likely they just stole it.

13 JANUARY

We have extra German classes now. It's one of the new laws our Nazi masters have brought in to try and turn us into good little Nazis. It won't work, of course – any more than anything else they've tried. They were very friendly when they first occupied our country. *Hey, we like your country. That's why we invaded it! Aren't you pleased? No? Why not?* Hardly anyone makes an effort in our German class now –

except Maarten, of course. I used to think this was because he wants to be best at everything, but now I wonder if it's because he secretly admires our German masters and wants to be like them. It's an uncomfortable thought, and I hope I'm wrong. Anneke and I never make any effort, of course. This morning, I opened my English book and we spent the whole lesson passing it back and forth, concealed inside our German translation. It amuses us to think how annoyed the Nazis would be if they knew.

I wouldn't mind if they'd ban maths! In our lesson today the teacher told me he'd suggest private tuition if he thought it'd do any good! He said it in front of the whole class, too. I felt as if he was deliberately setting out to humiliate me as he went over my workings. He even turned the book upside down to see if it made more sense that way! Anneke said I should take no notice. He's just mean, no one likes him, who cares about maths anyway and I'm good at lots of things. Like a best friend should. I know she wanted me to feel better, though it's a bit of a struggle to think what those things are. Mother says I'm untidy, and Pieter says I walk around with my eyes shut. But it made me feel even meaner that I was keeping a secret from Anneke. I don't know why I feel it is important I keep Jan secret. I just do.

After school was over I saw Maarten leave hand-in-hand with Saskia. Anneke says they've started going round together. Saskia's welcome to him. I haven't told Anneke my suspicions about him. I'd rather not think that we might have a fledgeling Nazi in our class. She asked if I'd like to join her and some other friends who were going to see a new film. It's an age since I've been to the cinema, so I did. I wish I hadn't. It was awful. I'd forgotten how bad the films are now they've been censored by the Nazis. Then just before it started a whole lot of soldiers came in and sat down in the row behind us and put their feet up on the seats. Of course no one dared to object. Anneke told me afterwards that she had a boot in her back all the way through.

Usually they put on a newsreel first. It's always propaganda, like what they write on posters and paste all round the town. About how wonderful the German Reich is and how brilliantly the War is going (if you're German). But this was something else. It was called "The Eternal Jew" and the lies it told made me feel really sick. The soldiers whistled and hooted but an old couple in front of us got up in disgust. But would you believe it? They were made to sit down again!

As soon as the main film began the soldiers began to talk. If I'd dared I'd have turned round and told them to be quiet. They act as if they own my country – and can behave just as they like. I felt really upset as we left. Anneke and I have made a pact now – no more films till the Germans are defeated.

I got home just in time to hear the daily broadcast from the BBC in London. I'd have been furious if I'd missed that on top of everything else. Each evening we're at home – which is nearly every evening these days – we settle down in comfy chairs around the radio. At eight o'clock Father switches it on and we listen out for the peep peep peep which tells us that the broadcast from London is about to begin. Of course it's against the Nazis' laws to listen to it, but no one takes any notice. We have a rule in our house that no one says a word till it is over. It's the only news we can rely on. When the news is glum – which it nearly always is these days – it comforts me to think that up and down the country there are countless families listening like us. We're all longing for news of the Allies Second Front, but it's being an awful long time in coming. But tonight, after seeing all those lies about the Jews I was desperate to hear something cheerful. Father asked why the long face, so I told him. He took my hands in his and said seriously that he was sure I knew it was all lies. I nodded. I just wish they wouldn't show it. There was a little question in Father's eyes, and I think I know why. It's as if drip by drip they're pouring propaganda into us to turn us against each other, but Father needn't worry about me. All that showing that film has done has made me hate the Nazis worse than ever, and made me determined to show the Jews by any means I can that I am on their side.

14 JANUARY

I'm an idiot! It's obvious why I haven't seen Jan at school. He's Jewish. There used to be a lot of Jewish boys and girls in my school, but they had to leave last September and go to separate Jewish schools. When we went back to school in the autumn it felt strange to see how our class had shrunk. The teachers tried to make it less obvious by taking out empty desks and chairs, but there was room to stretch out properly in the classroom, which there hadn't been before. I never see my Jewish friends now. At first I used to wonder what happened to them. Then I gradually forgot. Like you do. You get on with things. It's not that I don't care. But what choice do you have? Now, having seen that film, I wish I had made more of an effort. I suppose I didn't truly understand how bad things must be for them.

I don't suppose I'll ever see Jan again, and that makes me

feel a bit sad. There are so many things I'd like to ask him –
and now I never will. But I'm hanging on to that scarf – as a
keepsake of a special day. It will always remind me of him.